AGENTS OF VENGEANCE

AGENTS OF VENGEANCE

FEDERAL AGENTS OF MAGIC™ BOOK EIGHT

TR CAMERON   MARTHA CARR   MICHAEL ANDERLE

DISRUPTIVE IMAGINATION

Copyright © 2019 TR Cameron, Martha Carr and Michael Anderle
Cover Art by Jake @ J Caleb Design
http://jcalebdesign.com / jcalebdesign@gmail.com
Cover copyright © LMBPN Publishing
A Michael Anderle Production

LMBPN Publishing
PMB 196, 2540 South Maryland Pkwy
Las Vegas, NV 89109

First US edition, October 2019
eBook ISBN: 978-1-64202-489-0
Print ISBN: 978-1-64202-490-6

AGENTS OF VENGEANCE TEAM

Thanks to the JIT Readers

Dave Hicks
Diane L. Smith
Dorothy Lloyd
Larry Omans
Deb Mader

If we've missed anyone, please let us know!

Editor
The Skyhunter Editing Team

DEDICATIONS

For Dylan

— *TR Cameron*

To everyone who still believes in magic
and all the possibilities that holds.
To all the readers who make this
entire ride so much fun.
And to my son, Louie and so many wonderful friends who
remind me all the time of what
really matters and how wonderful
life can be in any given moment.

— *Martha*

To Family, Friends and
Those Who Love
To Read.
May We All Enjoy Grace
To Live The Life We Are
Called.

— *Michael*

CHAPTER ONE

The wind rippled through the forest and caressed Diana's face. Her foe stood between two tall, narrow trunks covered in mottled black-and-white bark, shaded by the broad leaves that created a canopy far above. Strange insects filled the surrounding air, entirely unlike those she was used to.

So, given that I've not been to ninety-nine percent of the places on Earth and even less of those on Oriceran, I must be... who the hell knows where? The breeze, which an author probably would have described as "playful," teased her by blowing her hair into her eyes. *Again.* She pushed it out of the way with a curse. *Could Fury have chosen a more annoying place for our training session?*

The sword continued to manifest in the imaginary worlds they shared as the same person she'd met in the virtual dojo during the trial. He wore his billowy black skirt, long enough to obscure his footwork, but had traded the grey tunic for a scarlet one this time. She didn't know if it was a personal choice on his part or a recognition of something she'd done.

I'm not sure of much where he's concerned when you come down to it. His face was narrow and sharp and his eyes and coloring always brought Japan to mind. *I wonder if there was a crossover between the planets long ago and that's the reason we have such variation in our ethnicities? I should ask someone about that. Professor Stanley, maybe.*

Her foe nodded his head, and the knot of inky hair on the top bobbed. He shouted to be heard above the rustle of the foliage and buzz of insects and across the fifteen feet that separated them. "Begin."

She immediately thrust forward to weave between the trees as he vanished from sight behind the trunks nearest him. Her tight ARES tunic and tactical pants stood strong against the attempts of the bark to slice her flesh, and her heavy boots crunched leaves and twigs with each stride. She drew her katana in a fluid motion and spun it once before her left palm joined the right on the hilt. Increasingly, she was now able to use the weapon without hand preference or conscious thought and the sword felt equally natural in either hand or both.

Cara had suggested—with no hint of sarcasm or humor —that she should have an MRI to chart the changes the blade was making in her brain. Then, unable to resist, the woman had broken into a grin and finished, "You know, if they have one sensitive enough to find something so small." Her second in command had fled the room before Diana could retort.

A flash of scarlet ahead and to the right drew her in that

direction, and she almost lost her head to the trap. Fury had selected his daisho for this bout and held the long sword in his right fist and the short sword in his left. It was the former—the tachi—that thunked into the trunk when she ducked under the backhand stroke barely in time while the latter sought to pierce her with a direct strike to her lowered throat.

She raised her own blade in a horizontal block, caught the tanto, and pushed it away. His skirt swished as he stepped toward her and she spread her legs wide to avoid a stamp to her shin, then rolled into a backward somersault to gain distance. She rose with her katana held in a diagonal cross-body guard and a smile stretched her lips.

Time to turn the tables.

Diana kicked forward to lift the dirt and debris from the forest floor and flurry it into her tormenter's face. His reaction was instinctive and he shied away to the left. She darted in and slashed down from above with a sharp cry. The katana glinted when it caught a stray beam of sunlight during its descent. He recovered quickly enough to bring the tanto across in a block before he spun to whip the tachi around in a backhand from the same side as he pushed her sword in the opposite direction. She went low again but forward this time, ducked, and stepped in. The weapon's sweep lifted her hair, and she brought her own blade up in a diagonal that reversed its original path and aimed to slice him from groin to left shoulder.

His move came as a surprise when he did a cartwheel flip in the direction of the stroke, fast enough to avoid the cut. *When did he become an acrobat? Dammit.* She was forced onto the defensive again as he used his paired blades to try to overwhelm her. The assault forced her to retreat and angle her own sword in block after block as she shifted it cleverly to disengage from one blade to counter the next.

When her back met the tree, she cursed herself for lack of awareness. She circled her katana in a wide swipe, then inward to catch two attacks and push both to her left. In the same fluid motion, she delivered a sidekick aimed at his ribs.

He took the blow, but his wicked speed manifested when he returned a kick to her planted leg's upper thigh and numbed the limb. She dropped involuntarily to that knee. He chopped down with a victory cry and a weapon drove in at an angle from each side to ensure she couldn't block both in time. She released the katana with her right hand and committed the blade to block the tachi on her left, longsword against longsword. At the same time, she wrapped her free hand in force and caught his tanto and the magic protected her from its edge.

His disapproval evidenced in a rapid shake of his head. "If it was a magical blade, you would have lost your hand."

She shrugged but her left arm shook as it fought to hold the block against the weapon he pushed toward her neck. "If it was a magical blade, I'd have blasted you into a tree instead of catching it."

Finally, he released, stepped back, and twirled his weapons once as he watched her rise. "You will not always have your magic. Remember the battle against the previous wielder."

"Of course." She frowned. "Why do I think you're playing me?"

His reply was a blur of motion, easily half again as fast as he'd attacked before. In the space between recognition and her body's instinctive response, the mental version of herself appeared on the periphery of her mind and shook her head above folded arms. *"Now you've done it."*

Sweat dripped into her eyes as she sidestepped behind a trunk, giving Fury the options of halting the chop that would have bisected her or burying the edge of his tachi in the tree. She hadn't realized there was a third choice until the blade glowed at the last instant and sliced through the obstacle as if it wasn't there. It scored a line of fire across her stomach that immediately started to fill with blood. The pain struck a moment later like acid poured on a strip of sunburn, but she was too busy diving out of the way of the falling tree to spare it any attention.

Diana scrambled to her feet and moved in a diagonal away from her foe and his Samurai fetish in an effort to position herself far enough away to collect her scattered focus. She wound a band of force around her torso to act as a pressure bandage on the cut, but it wouldn't hold for long. Since this was training and not a trial, she was sure her body was still unharmed in the customizable space in the back of the security agency. The area had suffered from disuse before she programmed it to empty out and put it to use during her sessions with the sword. *Almost sure. Okay, fairly sure.*

He caught up to her and their blades rang as they traded strikes, blocks, counters, and more blocks. The speed was faster than she'd ever experienced in the virtual world and far, far faster than any fight she'd had in the real one. He dealt her two more incisions, shallow but annoying, on her cheek and on her left arm. Worse, she didn't seem to be able to pierce his defenses with her sword.

Let's change it up, then. She spun and ducked under the slash from the tanto and lifted her katana to intercept his tachi, raising it high to entangle the swords so she could control his long blade for a moment. When he pulled the shorter one back to swipe it at her again, she fired a bolt of force at his chest. He bent backward almost in half to avoid it, but it gave her what she really needed—time to adjust.

Two more blasts were on the way as he straightened. He spun to dodge the first and slashed at the other with his tanto to boomerang it back at her. She sidestepped to evade it and waved a wide fan of fire at him while her mind protested. *He's not supposed to be able to do that.* He ducked under the flame, and she traded it for a hail of icicles before the other attack could start a wildfire. *Apparently, my use of magic freed him to do his own version of special annoying stuff. Cara was right. Sentient weapons can be jerks.*

He charged forward and slapped the frozen assault away with wide sweeps of the tachi and short slaps of the tanto. Infuriatingly, he wore the same grin he always did but at the moment, it seemed smug as well as slightly challenging. She ran at him, lead with her katana, and summoned a force blade in her other hand. They met in a clash of metal and magic and faced one another at close quarters, their noses an inch apart as each sought to overpower their opponent's defense. Sweat dripped down her torso and triggered more stinging pain from the wound on her stomach.

Okay, enough. She broke into a smile, drew her head back, and slammed her forehead into his nose. It crunched under the impact and he was sufficiently distracted that her blades slipped free. She stepped ahead and thrust her katana at his throat but only realized the tanto was in the way when it pierced her stomach.

The warehouse space materialized around her as Fury's laughter faded in her ears. It held a complimentary edge, though, as she would probably have survived her wound while he most certainly wouldn't have. She doubted the trick would ever work on him again. The physical sword in her real-world arms was heavy, and a trail of sweat glistened on the floor from her efforts.

She had watched a video replay of one of the sessions once and had been more than a little disconcerted to see herself run, jump, and swing as she battled an invisible opponent. Of course, she'd "fought" imaginary foes before in martial arts katas, but to watch her body doing it while her mind was off somewhere entirely different was trippy in the extreme.

A boot scuffed behind her, and she spun instinctively and raised the sword to high guard position—the hilt above her head and the blade angled slightly downward. Nylotte stood three feet away, her visage as dark as the black clothes she wore. Diana's face twisted in confusion. "How did you know where I was?"

The Drow rolled her eyes as if she'd asked the stupidest question available at that particular moment. "You are my protege. Why would I not know where you are?" She shook her mane of pale hair, which was unbound and inspired instant envy. "But your question is irrelevant, as usual. We have a problem that requires your immediate attention."

CHAPTER TWO

Diana stepped through the portal into Nylotte's basement, her hair still wet from a hasty shower and a change of clothes, She'd thrown gel in it and pushed it back from her face, but the Dark Elf had been adamant that she get there as quickly as possible because "One does not make Lady Alayne wait, however annoying she might be." She hadn't been sure whether her teacher had called her annoying or referred to the leader of the kemana but had concluded, while the water beat down on her tired muscles, that it was probably both.

She'd chosen her dressy leather jacket—a recent purchase that wasn't as heavily abused as the older one. Under it was a colorful top for a change to complement the dark tactical pants and spy boots. Technology had issues in the kemana, but she felt well-prepared with the throwing knives in the footwear. She'd practiced on the sly and tried and failed to keep up with Rath's impressive skills. Still, she was determined that someday, she would win a match against the troll.

The stairs creaked as she climbed to the main floor where her mentor sat in the chair she used when in trading mode behind the tall counter. The shop had been rebuilt to perfectly replicate the previous one, which had been destroyed during the recent unpleasantness in the kemana. Nylotte's motion was smooth and almost sinuous when she slid from the seat and curved around the edge to follow her student out the front door. It was purple-tinted daytime outside and the crystals high above cast their magical influence over everything below. The agent tilted her head upward and breathed in the pleasure of the magic's caress as it slowly bolstered the power reservoir within her.

She fell into step beside the Drow, who strode with purpose toward the castle at the end of the cavern. It was once pure white but scorch marks from the recent attack marred its perfect surface, visible even from a distance. The reminder of the battle brought a frown to her face. "So what's the deal, anyway?"

Nylotte didn't quite snort but her opinion was clear. "The lady of the kemana has demanded your presence and requested my help in making it happen."

"Demanded? Maybe I'll simply turn around and head back." Her eyes narrowed.

Her teacher chuckled. "Which is why I am involved. Alayne has not been herself since the attack. On the one hand, her increased attention to defense and rooting out those still enraptured by Rhazdon's message is a good thing. On the other, her manner has become equally aggressive toward friends and allies."

"I didn't realize you considered her your friend."

Another laugh held only wry amusement. "No, I'm in the latter category. The lady is far too uptight to ever be counted among my friends, and I am far too impertinent to be counted among hers."

She sent an overdeveloped look of shock at the other woman. "You? Impertinent? Surely such a thing cannot be."

"It's one feature we have in common. Speaking of which, did your hairdryer break?"

Diana growled, "You said it was urgent."

"I think you could have invested the three minutes to deal with it, given the complete lack of style you've chosen." It was true, unfortunately. After an enemy had sliced off a large section of hair, she'd had to opt for a short, messy coif. In practical terms, it was fantastic. It didn't stop her from being jealous of Nylotte's mane, however.

"Shut up."

The woman laughed once more as she waved at two Light Elves who passed them, a sickly sweet and clearly fake smile on her lips that dropped as soon as they were out of sight. She brushed her hands down the long black dress she'd donned—one that featured far too many vertical buttons and made her look like a warrior from ages past. *Which might actually be a legit description of her.*

"Such maturity you've gained during our months together." The sarcasm virtually dripped to the ivory stairs leading to the palace courtyard as they climbed them.

She stuck her tongue out, which confirmed her teacher's opinion, and frowned at the sight before them. "Why aren't there any guards?" The main entry before them was normally flanked by two exceptionally dour beings who held tall weapons and generally tried to appear threatening.

The Drow pointed to the right. "Because the doors were damaged during the battle and have been taken out of service. We need to use the small entrance." The path narrowed until the walls were so close, they could no longer walk side by side. A glance upward revealed rough-looking notches in the castle wall above, and her instincts suggested there were probably drawn bows behind them.

Damn. The Drow wasn't exaggerating. Lady Alayne is way more focused on defense than she was. They turned to the left and the expected sentinels appeared, guarding a much less impressive door between them.

The armored figures admitted them without discussion and one of them opened the barrier for them. They strode onto an uncarpeted hallway and their boots clicked against the polished stone. The elf she'd first met as the leader's emissary—and later discovered was also the woman's advisor and majordomo—stepped out from a side door to greet them. His brown hair was pulled back to display his pointed ears and accentuate the narrowness of his face. Whereas before, he had worn mainly dress robes, he was clad today in an ornate set of leather armor in complementary shades of black, emerald, and forest-green.

A thin smile appeared as he spoke to them. "Thank you for coming, Diana Sheen. Thank you for seeking her for the lady, Nylotte."

Her teacher nodded, and Diana restrained the snippy reply that had leapt to her lips and echoed the motion. He turned and led them deeper into the castle without speaking. She'd never seen this part of the building and was impressed with the tapestries on the wall that displayed ornate locations or battle scenes and on occasion, both. They arrived at a doorway and he ushered them through under the watchful eyes of another two guards, far more attentive and threatening than those outside the walls.

Inside was a much smaller version of the formal throne room, with the expected raised dais and ornamental seat. The leader of Stonesreach was perched upon it, clad in glimmering white leather and chainmail with gleaming jewels present on her hands, throat, ears, and brows. The Light Elf nodded at their arrival and settled her gaze on the agent. "Agent Sheen. Welcome back."

"Thank you, Lady Alayne. How may I be of service?"

The woman's mouth quirked slightly. "It seems as if we have a common cause. We were both in error, believing the threat was confined to the city above. With the assistance of your teacher, we have discovered many sympathizers within Stonesreach." Diana raised an eyebrow at Nylotte and the Dark Elf gave a hint of a nod. "Of course, we are dealing with them and I would not have requested your presence only for that."

The leader of the kemana shook her head and her beautiful golden hair spilled over the pale armor. "For some time, a powerful wizard on Oriceran has demanded that the kemanas swear fealty to him. Naturally, we have not done so here, although others have accepted oppression in return for peace. He has given us an ultimatum and threatened the destruction of our cities. Both of them. We are undeniably connected by this threat, and it would be wise for us to expand the relationship we have beyond one of response to one of open exchange."

She took several seconds to parse the woman's flowing speech before nodding. "Agreed, Lady Alayne. What did you have in mind?"

The elf raised a graceful hand. "A partnership in truth, where we share information freely."

The Drow spoke unexpectedly. "Is that truly something you are willing to do? To lower yourself to the level of the humans?" The snide tone in her voice and inflection suggested it was Stonesreach's ruler that the Dark Elf had doubts about.

The true meaning was clearly visible to the Light Elf, as well. She nodded gravely. "I am aware I have done much to earn criticism. But I am sincere in my offer. Full communication about any matters involving the wizard, the witch, or the believers."

Diana's brain translated quickly. *Lechnas, Iressa, or the Remembrance.* She was equal parts eager for and eager to avoid another showdown with the wizard who had claimed Rhazdon's Defense. On the other hand, she longed for a chance at retribution against the witch for her support of Sarah's insanity in her city. "I accept your offer. No secrets within the boundaries you have set."

A relieved smile appeared on the other woman's face, which made her look much younger and less confident than she had so far appeared. "Thank you, Agent Diana Sheen. If both of you are amenable, we could use Nylotte as a conduit for any news we wish to share."

They both looked at the Drow, who responded with a nod of confirmation. "I accept this burden. I would not wish the pain of mental communion with my student upon anyone else."

The agent sighed and Lady Alayne's smile grew larger. "Excellent."

It was clearly a dismissal, and the emissary ushered them from the room and from the palace with additional words of thanks. Once they were outside, she turned to her teacher and frowned at her. "Is it possible, ever, that you could manage not to insult me while we're around other people?"

The elf raised one of the pale eyebrows that stood out so noticeably against her dark skin. "Why would I wish to do such a thing? Being truthful is important. Now, I believe we have time for a training session, do we not?"

She sighed, rolled her aching shoulders, and wished she still had Fury with her to smack the Drow with. *Only the flat of the blade, that's all. And only once.* The expression on the other woman's face showed that she was fully aware of her student's feelings. She forced a bubbly tone into her voice, knowing it would annoy her. "Of course. There's nothing I'd enjoy more."

The scowl she received buoyed her spirits, but she knew the quip would result in that much more pain in the lesson to come.

CHAPTER THREE

The city at night was full of lights that winked at Rath where he was perched atop the Cathedral of Learning. His need to use that as a launch point in the recent past had revealed it as an excellent option, and he'd turned it into one of his primary locations by arranging to have a set of his gear always available on the roof. Fortunately, the elevators worked at all hours and the ID card Professor Charlotte had provided gave him access to the building whenever he needed it. If any of the security guards who saw him were concerned, they certainly didn't display it.

Probably think I'm a foreign-exchange student. He chuckled inwardly. The older folks who continued the memory of the Silver Griffins had explained the concept to him, and they'd all agreed there should be such exchanges between the two planets someday.

Tonight, though, he was not out for the Griffins or even on behalf of ARES. He still patrolled the city regularly, but that wasn't the objective for this adventure either. He had something else in mind, something far more dangerous but potentially very beneficial to everyone he cared about.

Simply put, he was hunting. His prey was the most perilous quarry he could imagine and the challenge would be to get close enough to talk without winding up dead in the process. The assassin Amadeo had access to his comm, but the communication was all one way. The troll had no means to reach out to him, which left him with only two options—wait, or act. The first wasn't his style, but the second was precarious in the extreme.

Danger is my middle name. Yeah, baby.

He pulled on his flight gear and transferred four of his throwing knives carefully into the rib sheaths he wore with it. A visit to Chan had provided a subtle poison for each that would cause drowsiness with any incision. He'd have to remember to throw only by the hilt, but the small risk was worth it. If the mysterious stranger took offense and turned aggressive, he'd need the edge. *Heh. Edge, get it?* He shook his head at himself. *Loopy troll is loopy.*

Satisfied that his preparations were in order, he pushed up to stand at the base of the tall spire that crowned the building and peered down over the city. His AI had worked on the problem for weeks and she had finally indicated only today that the probability was high enough to act. Despite that, he was still well aware of the potential negatives of his plan. He pushed them aside. *There's been nothing to suggest he might become our enemy. This shouldn't push him over the edge.*

"Show me, Gwen." A series of dots of varying sizes appeared as an overlay in his goggles. The larger ones were confirmed sightings of the man and the others were rumors or unexplained phenomena that his virtual assistant had decided were likely to be Amadeo. The circles decreased in size as the likelihood of a false positive increased.

It indicated that the graveyard Rath had initially discarded as being too obvious once the assassin invited him to it was actually his base of operations, and the invitation had almost certainly been intended to cause him to draw the conclusion that he had. Another clustered set of tiny points suggested a hidden entrance or exit on the far side of the steep hill that backed the location, which they'd agreed needed to be looked at whether they used it or not.

"Trajectory, please." A path in yellow—with arrows indicating the direction and rings identifying elevations— materialized. It would carry him over the graveyard at a high altitude and curve him around the far side of the hill. From there, he'd have the option to land or reverse course toward the cemetery again. He had no idea what he would do when he reached either of those places, other than hope for the best and wing it. *It's not a great plan, really.* Before he could overthink it, he leapt outward and set course for the closest glowing circle.

The wind whipped through his hair and the sheer pleasure of flying pulled a shout of joy from him as he curved through the first ring, aligned with the next, and caught an updraft to gain the altitude he'd lost. The streets and vehicles below resembled toy versions of themselves, and he imagined reaching down to move them from one street to the other. *Trollzilla.* Gwen added names to things that required his notice—like police cars or known troublemakers, the latter all fortunately accompanied by the men and women in blue on this evening. *Nothing to distract me from the mission.*

Another overlay was inserted into his visual field as the AI mapped the heat sources in the graveyard. It was his hope that it might be easy, that he'd simply see a warm body present among all the cold ones and settle beside it for a chat. Naturally, nothing was visible other than animal-sized blotches meandering with no clear indication as to what they were or why they were there.

Okay, we'll do it the hard way. He banked to make use of the wind channel for the push around the hill, then straightened before he curved along his path on the opposite side. Again, there was no heat source to home in on, but Gwen increased the magnification of his goggles as the suspected entry came into sight. Sure enough, he could see a wrought-iron gate that appeared rusty and disused covering what looked like a large drainpipe.

"Is the ground extra wet?" They'd had a little rain in the past couple of days, so even though most areas were dry, if this was a place where water was channeled off the hill, there should be some evidence of it.

"Negative."

He grinned. *All right, then, so it's something other than drainage. Worth taking a look at.* "Landing path, please." A blue line and rings appeared in his display, and he arced rapidly to fly into the prevailing breeze instead of with it to circle downward slowly and safely. When he was a few feet from the ground, he pressed the switch that lay on the crossed straps on his chest and the wings collapsed into the rectangular box on his back. He landed softly to crouch and listen to be sure no one had noticed his approach.

Satisfied that no enemies were about, he straightened. "Gwen, analyze the grate." His visual display flickered as she ran sonic, heat, and energy tests on it, and the AI discovered exactly what he'd hoped for—hinges and a locking device. She sounded satisfied at the discovery. "Electronic lock. I won't be able to break it."

Rath shrugged out of his gear and set it aside carefully. He slid the goggles, batons, belt, and knife vest through the gaps in the crossbars, which were too small for most people but adequate for those items. He'd considered simply assuming his largest form and ripping the grate off, but that would be both noisy and impolite so he'd rejected the idea. Instead, he shrank as far as required, skipped through the opening, and grew back to his three-foot size on the opposite side.

When he had geared up once more, he moved ahead into the darkened pipe in a crouch. The low-light function of his goggles rendered everything in greys and greens. The air smelled clean and fresh and discounted any possibility that the tunnel was still used for its original purpose. He paused with his foot in midair when his instincts screamed a warning and stepped back instead of forward. After a moment, he got down on all fours, his stomach barely off the concrete of the pipe floor, and peered into the gloom until he finally identified a thin black piece of wire at ankle height. It disappeared into the wall, but he was sure it would lead to something nasty if it was Amadeo's work.

"Gwen, infrared and laser detection?" A crisscrossing array of lines appeared in his goggles beyond the tripwire. Rath shook his head. *If he's this paranoid, he probably knows someone is coming.* He felt anxiety building and paused to think the situation through before he decided to persevere because the outcome was so important. "Keep scanning for everything and show in my display."

His vision became a mess of distractions, but he forced himself to focus through them. The easy way would be to shed his equipment and proceed at his smallest size, which would allow him to pass under most of the obstructions. As a bonus, the man would clearly know he wasn't a threat under those circumstances.

He had almost decided to do it when an alternate thought came to him—that it was a choice the assassin would never make for himself and might see as a weakness in another. It pushed him across the line to the decision he favored, which would be more fun and far more dangerous.

The troll checked to ensure all his items were secured, took six steps back, and darted forward. He jumped the first trap and hurdled the second. With a slide, he avoided the third and turned his motion into a sideways roll to tuck between two horizontal detectors. He landed on his palms and toes in a push-up above a red channel that passed beneath his suspended body. Rath climbed carefully to his feet, made one more diving somersault through the diamond-shaped opening ahead of him, and rolled smoothly to his feet.

There were no more visible sensors, but his suspicions were on high alert. "Gwen, more light on the floor." Both the illumination and the graininess of the image increased and brought an area suspiciously devoid of footprints into view. Looking ahead, he saw a pattern. *Pressure-sensitive probably. Very tricky, but not for a troll.* While the plates were positioned to be triggered by a full-sized human walking normally, his smaller stature and agility made them fairly easy to negotiate.

The path continued but there was an opening to the right. *Looks like it was broken through, not too long ago.* He stuck his head around and immediately saw the assassin seated on a large wooden crate, watching the entrance. His undisguised voice held a mixture of irritation and amusement. "Come on out, Rath. If I'd wanted you dead, I would have collapsed the pipe with you inside. You failed to see the motion detectors outside the gate."

Dagnabit, dang, and drat. He moved warily through the opening and into a wide room made of stone with marble accents and illuminated by harsh work lights on stands directed at the walls and ceilings. A generator hummed softly in the corner. "What is this place?"

Amadeo's black mask hid his face but amusement was audible in his words. "My estate, such as it is. Most people aren't able to enjoy their mausoleum until they're dead. Me, I get double value from it."

Rath's head tilted in disbelief. "Really?"

He shrugged. "No, but it's a poetic thought, isn't it? The family that built it doesn't need it for a while as long as nothing unexpected happens. My research revealed this basement, which was added without their knowledge as a utility space for the drainage system and promptly forgotten when the city resolved the water challenge in a different way. It's perfect for me, now that I've sealed the other exit."

That is a lie. Not a chance you left yourself only one escape route. "Nice secret lair."

The man laughed but sobered quickly. "If anyone other than you had come down that pipe, they'd be dead."

"Did you disarm traps?"

"No." He stood from the crate and walked forward slowly. "If you couldn't make it on your own, you didn't deserve to make it at all. It's kind of a metaphor for life, you know?"

"Needed to talk to you."

The assassin stopped and hooked his hands in his belt. He was in the only outfit Rath had ever seen him in—entirely black and equipped for combat. For whatever reason, he truly was a mystery, which was essentially why the troll was there. His tone had become less aggressive and more interested as they'd talked, which was encouraging. "Why?"

The troll crossed the distance between them to stand a couple of feet away. "Remembrance. Really gone? You would know best."

"That is a very intelligent question." He pointed a gloved finger. "You have good instincts, my friend." The compliment was followed by a much less welcome statement. "But why should I help you? First, you invaded my sanctuary and disturbed my peace. Second, if anyone saw your entrance, you've likely consigned them to death by having a hillside dropped on them."

He shrugged. "You care. About Griffins. About innocents." *About me, for some reason.* The assassin stood unmoving, his eyes invisible behind the black plastic. Each tick of the clock added tension to the moment, and his fingers itched to check that his blades were ready to be drawn. Finally, the mask dipped in a nod.

"We've reached the limits of my caring, troll. If you try to come back here, things will go badly for you. Do you understand?" He answered with his own nod, and the man backpedaled to the crate and sat again. "The Remembrance is not entirely destroyed. Someone new has backed the bounties on your friends."

"Idea who?"

"No, which is concerning to me professionally, regardless of our connection. Not that I'd be interested in claiming them, anyway. But there are definitely things moving in the city's shadows. Homes of some notable magic users have been broken into and items of power stolen. It seems there is still someone trying to collect magical things, but their identity has not yet been revealed." He spread his hands to the sides. "It certainly sounds like the new boss is the same as the old boss, doesn't it?"

Rath nodded. "Won't get fooled again."

The assassin let a chuckle escape. "The actual lyric is more appropriate. See that you 'Don't get fooled again.'"

"Any ideas on where to start?"

There was a hint of frustration in the man's voice when he replied. "Not really. Things are still upside down from your attack on them. Good job, by the way, although you missed at least one person. I watched him run before you got there."

The troll frowned. *Who escaped? How did Amadeo know to watch?* But he doubted the man would share any more information without expecting something in return, so he let it pass. "Easier way out?"

"No. Earn it. Also, if you seek me out again, we will no longer be friends. And, trust me, you do not want to cross that line. If I hear anything you need to know, I will contact you."

"Thank you."

"Go."

He retraced his steps and avoided all the traps very cautiously as he retreated. When he was on the far side of the gate again—having checked carefully to be sure no one would see him when he emerged—he exhaled a sigh of relief. He opened one of the pouches that had been left behind and extracted two wands he'd snagged on the night of the battle. They clattered on the concrete of the pipe as he tossed them inside the grate. It was a gesture, nothing more, but he knew of no other way to offer his thanks in a fashion that wouldn't offend the assassin.

That done, he looked up, judged that the hill would be sufficiently high to give him enough lift to fly home, and started to climb.

CHAPTER FOUR

When Sloan had finally abandoned his undercover persona and rejoined the team, he had destroyed everything associated with Tommy Ketchum, exactly like he always did at the end of an op. It was a ritual that let him fully separate his personality and truly become Sloan again.

One of the items, however, lived on in electronic form. Kayleigh had taken the sim chip from the cell phone he'd used with the gang and Deacon had duplicated it virtually and stored it on a server far away from the base. It had been as much "because we can" as "just in case," but he hadn't felt like arguing with the techs. The physical device was gone and it had been banished from his mind with the other trappings of his undercover personality.

The separation had lasted until an hour before, when Kayleigh had pinged his new phone with a text message they'd received on the old one. It had simply named a time and a place, using shorthand he'd shared with the man who sent it. In the back of his mind, Sloan had hoped that Mur had found a way out of the mess of the Remembrance, and it was good to discover that he was at least still alive.

Diana had given him the go-ahead to proceed as he saw fit—with proper precautions. He was wired with a backup microphone threaded into his hair and a locator beacon in the heel of his shoe in case his comm was taken or needed to be sacrificed to build trust. Kayleigh would listen in from the base, and Hank was already in position in a bar around the corner from the target location.

He swung the SUV into the parking lot of the Thai restaurant in the city's affluent Shadyside district. The choice was a subtle confirmation that the person on the other end of the line was Murray because he'd often mentioned his love of the place. Sloan stepped out of the vehicle and stretched, using the motion as cover to survey the area for enemies. None were evident—no witches, wizards, or antagonistic humans lurked in the corners that he could see, so reassured, he strode toward the entrance.

There was a typical lunchtime crowd inside, but he saw his companion immediately. Mur appeared smaller—as if the stress of the recent past had burned away some of his flesh—but was still dressed impeccably in black from top to toe. A bottle of beer sat at his right hand, and he toyed with a phone with his left. He looked up when the agent arrived and his expression shifted seamlessly from relief to anger to pain. Mur banished the feelings with a shake of his head that returned his features to neutral and gestured at the chair across from him.

The big man spoke as Sloan sat and emotion thickened his voice. "So first, thank you. For the meeting…and for the other thing."

He nodded, appreciating the sensitivity. The other thing was a warning he had sent from a throwaway phone minutes before the ARES agents raided the warehouse. He'd used another piece of shorthand they'd developed during the time Marcus was at his most crazy to tell him to drop everything and run.

His greatest fear during the battle had not been taking damage or being killed but seeing his friend—Tommy Ketchum's friend—in the crosshairs and having to decide yet again whether to kill him or not. It was a breach of tradecraft and security that was unprecedented in his career. He still couldn't quite put his finger on why he'd done it, only that it had felt like the right choice in the moment. *Maybe that's why I've always kept a burner handy.* "I'm glad things worked out."

Mur nodded. "So, you're not really Tommy Ketchum, then."

"I was, for a time. But no, not anymore."

"Can I ask your real name?"

He shrugged. "Sloan."

There was a pause while the man in black ran the response through his mind, the process obvious in his expression. Finally, he shrugged. "Tommy's a better handle for you."

Sloan laughed. "Maybe it is. But good old 'Ketch' is no more."

"So you worked for the other side all along?"

"Yep." He sighed, leaned back in his chair, and gestured for the approaching server to get them both bottles of beer. "Undercover intelligence. They didn't need to turn me. It's my job."

"You do it well." His voice held an edge of pain that cut into the agent's soul but he forced the sympathy away. *This is what I do.* "I couldn't believe it in the warehouse. I would never have guessed." He shook his head. "Did anyone else know?"

"No one on your side."

Mur chuckled. "Ouch. It kinda hurts when you say it like that."

He grinned at the appearance of what he thought of as the real Murray. It was something he'd seen often when they were together in a small group of people but never at the warehouse. "Yeah, I get that. It kind of hurt when you wanted to kill me, too."

The waiter arrived at that instant and forestalled a reply as they each ordered Pad Thai. Sloan chose a medium heat, sticking with a five, and looked around the dining room while Murray discussed levels with the server. Windows covered a side wall and the far wall, and pale pink drapes filtered the midday sun. A row of tables stood down the center with booths on both long sides of the narrow rectangle that comprised the restaurant. Black vinyl was the main material, with matching plastic tabletops and accents in gold and scarlet everywhere. A dragon stretched the length of the wall to his right, with glistening scales in jewel tones and a wicked grin on its face. Finally, the big man decided on spiciness level eight, and the server scurried away.

Murray sighed. "In the moment, I couldn't process it and I acted on instinct. I'd do it differently if I had the chance."

Sloan nodded. He'd read the conflict in the other man's

mind with his magic and had revisited the episode several times since. The response had been all action, Mur's ability to think knocked away by the magnitude of Tommy Ketchum's betrayal. "I wish I was able to say the same. But you were mixed up with some bloody awful people."

"Yeah. You know, though, I was never a true believer. It was merely a business opportunity." He paused before he barked a single laugh. "Yes, I'm aware of how bad that sounds."

He couldn't contain his own chuckle. "Well, as long as you're aware."

The big man raised his gaze and locked it on his companion's. "Seriously. Thank you. I didn't deserve it."

The agent shook his head. "You did. You were the best of them and tried at every turn to take the situation in the least damaging direction possible. If it had been you in charge instead of that maniac Marcus, things could have gone very differently."

"Maybe." Mur shrugged. "Or maybe the power would have been too much. It's probably good that we'll never find out. Anyway, I didn't only ask you here to say thanks and rehash old times. I heard something I thought you might like to know."

"And we had to meet for you to share it?"

"Actually, yes." The look in his eyes was honest and open. "I had to see that beneath it all, you were the same person I remembered. And you are—or are at least close to it."

He inclined his head in acknowledgment. "Fair enough."

"The crazy witch—may she rest in pieces and eternal pain—wasn't the person in charge. Her boss was someone called Iressa. I went back to the warehouse and found information in one of Vincente's hidden places I knew Sarah was aware of."

And we apparently missed. Well done us. "We had a lead that she wasn't the top of the food chain but not who was above her."

Mur sighed. "I assume 'we' is the group the rest of us constantly fought against?" Sloan nodded. "No wonder they were so much trouble." They both laughed at that. *Our world is a weird one, no doubt about it.* "Anyway, this Iressa apparently had crazypants work on something that involved a large number of explosives."

Their food arrived, and Mur dug in before Sloan could reply. He nibbled at his own meal and kept his gaze on the other man for an opportunity to speak without disturbing his evident enjoyment of his food. The spice was everything that was promised and soon, his tablemate sweated and called for a refill of his drink. Finally, he took a break and leaned back with a satisfied sigh. "Damn, that is some good stuff."

He laughed. "You'll have no argument from me. I'm glad you chose this place. But back to our discussion—is there anything else you have to share?"

The other man shook his head. "Nothing really, only that the explosives were apparently acquired and hidden somewhere. There was no indication of where. It was only a financial record." He laughed despondently. "It turns out she was skimming somewhat enthusiastically."

"I've seen pictures of her condo. That makes sense."

Mur wiped his face with the napkin to clear the last of

the spice-induced sweat. "It's always the ones in charge who screw things up, you know?"

"Yep. That is so true."

The big man rose and extended a hand. "Sloan, it was nice to see you. Thanks again. For everything."

He stood and gripped it warmly. "That goes both ways, Mur. You looked out for me, and I appreciated it. I still do. It could all have been much worse."

Murray gave a vague nod and broke the connection, then ambled out the building's front door. "Let him go," Sloan said, knowing the others would hear his instruction and would likely obey. The flash he'd received while they shook wasn't as deep as the one in the warehouse had been, but there was no recrimination in the man toward him. They might not be friends, but they definitely weren't enemies. Which, all things considered, was an improvement.

He threw a few bills on the table and headed to the SUV. Once he slid into the vehicle, his comm activated and Kayleigh's voice broke the stillness. "Get back here. The boss wants to talk about the explosives." He sighed and pulled out into the traffic, wondering what the crazy witch's last plan had been and whether someone was still around to carry it out for her.

CHAPTER FIVE

D iana was driving angry, frustrated after the meeting with Sloan to discuss the new revelation. She'd used her car that morning simply for the pleasure of being behind the wheel, but the hard turns and quick accelerations she normally enjoyed on the way home did little to make her feel better about life. In fact, the abundance of idiots on the road soured her already questionable mood.

"Get out of the fast lane, idiot," she yelled inside the closed windows, glad that Rath wasn't there to see her lose her cool. She pressed down the accelerator and the car surged forward barely in time to speed through the changing light and she noticed the black-and-white police vehicle only as she hurtled past. With a muttered curse, she flicked her gaze to the rearview mirror to verify that it hadn't decided to follow her and turned onto a back way home in case the officer behind the wheel felt it would be worth it to pursue the Mustang.

That's some annoying junk I absolutely don't need tonight.

A few turns later, she was sure she'd avoided any potential interaction with the authorities. She coasted to a stop in the parking lane on a tree-lined road, put the car in park, and leaned back with her eyes closed. *This was supposed to get easier once the damn Remembrance was taken care of. Why am I still dealing with their nonsense?* No answers were forthcoming, and she contemplated restarting her trip when her phone buzzed with a text.

It was from Bryant, inviting her to dinner at a hole-in-the-wall restaurant they both loved on the north side of the city. She sent him a flirty message back and he responded with appropriate emoticons declaring love and suggesting a night of romance. It wasn't his usual, but it brought a smile to her face.

Look at that. Bry-Bry is loosening up a little. Imagine. She accepted the invitation, shoved the car into motion, and headed home to get ready, her mood already much improved and getting more so by the mile.

She showered hurriedly and applied her makeup, then stood in front of her closet and stared at her clothes. It wasn't a fancy eatery, so the small right-hand portion devoted to dresses was irrelevant. It wasn't a nightclub, so the opposite side dedicated to far slinkier dresses and tops was also unnecessary. She looked down the middle for something that called her name and pushed hangers aside one by one before she realized that maybe the garments on the left had potential. After a moment's deliberation, she selected shiny leather pants still new enough to creak on occasion and a bright red blouse that was sufficiently tight to accentuate her curves but not so much as to put them on display. *Well, not totally on display, anyway.*

Once dressed, she turned her attention to her hair, Nylotte's criticisms having inspired her to pay more regard to it of late. She spiked the top upward and slicked the sides back to create a more dramatic style than she usually adopted. *Once he sees this, Bryant will be very thankful he asked me out.* She checked her watch and cursed and dropped onto her bed to pull her spy boots on—the right one with a stiletto down the back and throwing knives on either side and the left with the stiletto and the holster for her backup gun. A look in the mirror caused her to growl at the bulge of the revolver, poorly hidden by the tight leather pants, and changed the boots for the newer pair that traded the Ruger for another brace of throwing knives.

She looked at her reflection again and nodded. *Much better.* She snatched up her clutch purse as she ran to the door and yelled goodbye to Rath, who had his eyes glued to a *Star Trek* movie on the couch with Max. Chris Pine was on the screen, so it was one of the newer ones, which was good since the idea of him quoting Shatner was almost too painful to bear. She slid into the car and started the engine. The timing was about right to get her there at the appointed moment if traffic was light and she drove fast. *Or if it's heavy and I drive faster.* She pressed the accelerator with a smile and swung into combat with the city's rush hour.

Thankfully, she found a place to parallel park a couple of blocks from the restaurant, checked her lipstick a final time, and stepped out and closed the door. It wasn't the best neighborhood. Many of the windows were protected with bars and all the businesses lowered gates and grates overnight, but when she looked around, no potential trouble drew her attention. The sun had begun to slip behind the buildings and cast long shadows across her path as she walked downhill toward her destination.

There was a maker-space on the way, two storefronts that had been merged into a community center with tools and computers and printers and such. Inside was a class of some kind led by a white-haired woman in a long cardigan. The students represented a wide variety of ages and skin colors and leaned in eagerly to hear what the teacher had to share. The sight made her smile.

If only all of us could get along so well, the world would be a very different place. Both worlds, probably.

The front of the restaurant was a brick wall with crumbling mortar in the seams and *Antony's* painted in flowing script that was faded in several places. Graffiti had been added to the bricks but to the credit of the neighborhood, it was an accent to the sign. First, someone had outlined it, and another person, to judge by the style, had contributed symbols and designs to create a little spice. Something had been covered over in one corner, and she imagined a nightly battle of paint cans fighting for dominance. The changing images were one of the things she and Bryant liked about the eatery. She checked her watch again, noted that she was a few minutes late, and headed to the door to see if her date was waiting.

It swung open to reveal the small lobby with the cash register and the *Please wait to be seated* sign. She complied with the written instruction with a smile on her face. The public portion of the restaurant was square, filled half the block in the direction she'd come from, and stretched an equal distance to the back. Two rows of booths were separated by one of four-tops on the lower level, and the higher level was the same, minus the tables, a few steps up. She scanned the larger than usual crowd in search of Bryant and found him waving at her from the far corner of the upper area.

Changing it up. Cool. The owner hadn't emerged to seat her yet but they were friends so she felt comfortable breaking the rules. She headed forward and had barely cleared the top step when everything around her slipped into slow motion.

Diana realized belatedly that the band on her wrist had grown colder and had now begun to hurt where it rested against her bare skin. She went with the failsafe option devised during combat with Nylotte and sheathed herself in a cocoon of ice that didn't actually touch her body. Force blasts pounded it, fire washed over it, and throwing knives stabbed into it but failed to penetrate far enough to threaten her safety. Her first instinct was to sprint to Bryant so they could deal with the attack together, but his features were already in mid-dissolve and transformed into something different. She cursed. *Jarkko again. Damned Dwarf.*

She spun within the rapidly dwindling cocoon and faced the front to chart her path toward the door. During the turn, she identified more dwarves, wizards, and witches and at least a handful of Kilomea as well. *The little bastard invited everyone to this party.* The time was almost right to move when the gates and grates descended with a crash and the locks clicked into place to block every egress from the restaurant's dining room.

Fear washed through her but vanished equally as quickly when one of Rath's favorite expressions leapt into her mind. "Fear leads to the dark side." Imagining the three-foot-tall purple-haired troll imitating the two-foot-tall green-skinned Jedi Master filled her with warmth, as it always did, and made her grin despite the situation.

Okay, assholes. Let's dance.

CHAPTER SIX

I n the few seconds available to her, Diana tapped her comm to activate her microphone and stated, "Ambush, roll anyone near." The instant responses that should have followed failed to materialize, confirmation that the elaborate trap had taken her ability to communicate into account. More attacks struck the shield around her, and the dwarf had created a focused cone of flame that was mere seconds from burning through her cocoon. It had already created cracks that stretched toward one another on the inner surface. She kept an eye on them so she could duck when they met and let the beam through and tried to cast a portal at her feet.

She'd almost summoned the rift when the spell wavered and failed to finish. *I am Jack's complete lack of surprise.* Sadly, she couldn't eliminate whoever prevented her escape as there was no obvious target. *It could be any of these bastards.* She marshaled her force magic and released it in a wave to shatter the ice and hurl jagged shards throughout the dining room. The assault flung the closest foes from their feet, but those farther back raised hasty but effective defenses against the projectiles.

A sharp gesture with her hand delivered a cone of ice at the dwarf that would have reached him if he hadn't ducked under the table to avoid it. There was no time to wait for him to reappear, as enemies on both levels had already moved in to kill her. She ran at a diagonal toward the railing that separated the high area from the lower one and an arrangement of gaudy brass pipes she prayed were less flimsy than they appeared. A leap took her to the top, where she shifted her weight and vaulted again, away from the lobby where they'd expect her to go and toward the far side of the restaurant. Three lines of lightning intersected with a loud snap in the place she'd vacated.

A Kilomea's eyes widened as she careened toward him. He raised a paw to swipe her aside but it wasn't nearly powerful enough to stop her from planting her boot in his chest and landing on top of him as he fell. She stamped down, crushed his nose with her heel, and spun to face the other the attackers. Her movement in a direction other than the safety of the room's exit had surprised most of her enemies, who still tried to turn to reacquire her. The most alert in the group fired a blast of shadow from her wand.

The agent growled at the appearance of the variety of magic she despised above all — *although illusion has moved up the list damn fast*—and summoned a force shield to absorb it. *A necklace of magical deflectors for formal occasions...that's what I need. I wonder if Kayleigh can put that together for me.* She caught the cone on the buckler and kept it aligned as she jumped onto one of the tables in the booths along the restaurant's street-side wall.

The appearance of an opponent in the seat in front of her was a shock. He rose but she had time to lift a boot and block his wrist, which held a long dagger aimed at her thigh. The action caused her to slip and she dropped the clutch purse she'd forgotten she had to balance herself with her right hand on the wall. It provided stability for the kick that planted the toe of her boot in the dwarf's mouth that had opened, possibly for a victory screech. His teeth shattered and his skull snapped against the padded vinyl-covered wood hard enough to make his eyes roll to white.

Regrettably, the pleasure from the strike was short-lived. Her attack had sacrificed momentum and a force blast flung her into the wall. Her instinctive curl ensured that the blow to the back of her head was light enough to only screw her vision up slightly, rather than steal her consciousness. Five apparently airborne Kilomea resolved into one a second before the huge female collided with her.

The good news was that the charge carried her out of the path of two thrown weapons and a fireball, although the latter licked at her flesh as she tumbled over the high-backed booth in front of her. The bad news followed moments later when the giant creature landed on her and Diana thunked face-first into the next table in the row. It supported them for only an instant before its spindly legs and wall anchor failed, and the bulk of her opponent all but pulverized her for a second time when they landed on the floor.

Her breath was gone, lost in one of the collisions, and her wits were scattered from the intensity of the attack.

She registered that her left arm was bent beneath her, and enough pain radiated from it that it was probably broken. The right was extended before her and unchecked, so she moved her head to the side and aimed back and up to fire the wicked darts of flame that were Cara's favorite magic at her foe.

The Kilomea shrieked when they struck—hopefully somewhere sensitive—but the weight didn't diminish. *Shit, we're trapped between the booths so there's nowhere to go.* She looked up hastily. A dwarf sprinted toward her and looked for all the world like a football player about to launch a kick that would send the ball—her face, in this particularly unfortunate instance—into the stratosphere.

The giant above her continued to writhe and howl and to grind her immense weight onto the broken arm. Something else gave in the limb and tears trickled from the corners of the agent's eyes as she worked her free hand under her again. Literally seconds before the dwarf lashed his foot at her, she triggered a blast of force that lifted both her and the Kilomea upward and pounded them against the ceiling. In the instant of separation when they began to fall again, she managed to push herself out from under the huge creature with another burst of force magic. She landed in a momentarily empty location farther from the door but closer to the purse she'd dropped and the healing potion that lay within.

She scrambled to it and fumbled the container out with her functioning hand, then rose to spin away from a thin beam of fire aimed at her head. A distant part of her brain that still maintained the capacity for thought noticed that the interior of the restaurant was now aflame in several places. She had no time to deal with it and instead, popped the top of the vial with a thumb and raised it to her lips. The cool liquid trailed across her tongue and she braced for the rush of pain and pleasure that defined magical healing.

A thrown dagger knocked the flask out of her grip, spilled the contents on the floor, and inspired the most venomous curse she could come up with. The tiny amount she'd taken healed the arm only enough that it changed from numb back to full feeling, which was definitely not an improvement.

Diana waved her right hand in a wide arc to summon a curved barrier of ice that reached from floor to ceiling to protect the corner she inhabited. Her magic wasn't powerful enough to blast through the wall in one attempt, so she discounted that option. *I gotta get out of the kill zone.* The translucent sheet had already almost failed in places under a concerted attack and her arm throbbed. On any other day, a good fight might have been welcome given her earlier mood. That aside, she'd still have preferred the original plan of a date with Bryant rather than battling a horde of magical creatures bent on her destruction.

When she blasted the ice away like she had before, it had minimal effect because the enemy had seen that tactic already and had prepared their defense. She raced toward two wizards who stood where the tables had been before combat had destroyed or repositioned them but also kept track of the figures on the upper level in her peripheral vision.

Now that she'd begun to move, her back was exposed and she couldn't afford to stop. She used her telekinesis to steal the first one's wand and offered a prayer of thanks when her oldest trick actually worked. A gesture whipped the slender piece of wood across his partner's eyes with a solid smack. He howled and fell while she careened into the first at full speed, leading with her undamaged shoulder to sprawl him into a booth.

She spun awkwardly to raise her right hand in line with the upper level. A force blast redirected a leaping Kilomea onto a new trajectory that carried him into the wall and dropped him atop the wizard Diana had bowled over. The lack of balance induced by her useless arm made her stumble as she turned toward her original path, and she barely managed to deflect two daggers aimed at her chest with a force-covered forearm.

The raised block left her open, and the dwarf who had thrown the first two weapons had launched a delayed third she hadn't seen coming. It stabbed into her flesh below her collarbone, mere inches above her heart. The pain was immense but she didn't dare to take the time to pull it out or risk the potential bloodletting doing so would cause. She screamed in anger and agony and engulfed him in flame. He summoned a magical defense to protect himself but it wasn't sufficient against her follow-up attack—a boot that snapped all the momentum of her frantic run into his groin. With an immensely satisfying screech, he collapsed in a mewling heap.

The restaurant was strangely arranged, a point she never failed to point out to the owner. The only access to the kitchen was down a hallway on the side farthest from the dining room, which required the servers to weave through any customers who hadn't yet been seated. Antony had shrugged it off and simply said, "Builds character," in his thick Italian-flavored English. She'd never been sure whether the accent was legitimate or assumed but either way, it always made her laugh.

Now, that floor plan would serve her well if she could reach the corridor, barring any other enemies who might be inside waiting for her. Only a single being stood between her and her objective—a massive Kilomea with a battle-ax in one hand, a long sword in the other, and an expression on his face like he'd actually won the lottery. He filled most of the lobby with his bulk and the curved counter that held the cash register and various sweets for sale seemed to be the only thing that prevented him from filling it entirely.

Diana's mind blanked, overwhelmed by the situation and the pain that radiated from wounds both large and small, and instinct assumed control. Her body charged the giant and angled toward the door to entice him to move in that direction and away from the hallway that led to the rear section of the restaurant. When he shifted to intercept her, she used a force blast to hurl herself up and over the cash register, but his reflexive swing of the battle-ax caught her as she rocketed past. The sharpened point ripped a line down her side and slashed a hole in both her top and her flesh from ribs to waist.

A neutral voice in her head observed, *"Flesh wound. Shallow. Ignore it,"* so she did. In mid-air, she saw Jarkko appear from under his invisibility illusion where he stood beside the door they'd expected her to try to reach. *Traps behind traps. Competent fucking bastard.* Her boots struck the floor on the other side of the lobby and she thumped into the wall and raced for all she was worth down the short corridor that led to the single-door entrance to the kitchen.

Safety was two feet away when a force blast hammered her in the back and hurled her off her feet.

CHAPTER SEVEN

Again, her instinct to curl in a protective ball when threatened saved her. The blast lifted her and hurtled her toward the door. Rather than impact it with her face, she struck it with her shoulder and continued through. She landed in a heap and immediately skittered to her feet in a dizzy panic, then spun and layered ice and force over the entrance to give her a moment to collect the fragmented pieces of her mind.

It won't hold them for long, but at least it's something. She darted to the back exit but realized the enemy had prepared well enough that more of them probably lurked on the other side. She used her magic to move several heavy appliances in front of it and built a barrier three deep. The cost of maintaining the defenses would drain her eventually, but hopefully not before help arrived.

Diana stumbled to the supplies area in the back and found plastic wrap and duct tape. She ripped off a piece of each, using her teeth to tear the tape from the roll, before she set them on the counter. A convulsive jerk with her right hand ripped her blouse where the knife protruded. She locked her jaw, took a deep breath, and yanked the blade out with a shout of pain before she threw it aside and snatched up the wrap in a single motion. Her hands shaking, she pushed the clear plastic over and into the wound and slapped the tape over it before the welling blood could push it free. Although her body longed for rest, she forced herself to move instead and panted as she returned to the front of the kitchen.

The shields over the entrance had almost failed by the time she arrived, and she looked hastily around her for options. On her right as she faced the door was a dishwashing station, with plates in racks ready to be packed into the machine. The long cooking line was positioned on her left and a metal counter separated the cooks from the wait staff. Pots and pans rested on every surface on the far wall, as did the other utensils that a professional chef required to do their job. The narrow space in the middle was only wide enough for two people to pass, which must have been deeply annoying for the restaurant's employees. Or one Kilomea, as became evident when her barrier fell and the hulking brute from the lobby stepped through.

High sections of raised counter on both sides hindered him as he rushed to the attack. The battle ax's curved blade sliced down at a shallow angle, and she pivoted away to avoid it. His longsword stabbed forward, and she caught it with a force-shielded hand and launched a rapid inside-out crescent with her front foot to knock it from his grip.

He snarled and whipped the ax at her head. The blow chopped through one of the shelf supports on the right and a pile of plates cascaded to shatter on the floor. She ducked under the swipe, raised a palm as she stood, and thrust it at him in a command for the broken shards to rise and pepper his face. He raised a huge paw in time to protect his eyes but sustained a few bloody gashes on his forehead and jaw.

She grinned when an idea occurred to her and swept her arm wide to summon the rest of the scattered kitchen implements. The Kilomea backpedaled and did his best to block the pots, pans, dishes, and trays that bombarded his head. While he was distracted, she reached out with her power for the knives arranged in a long line above the cooking station and hurled them at his stomach. Some struck hilt-first and clattered harmlessly to the floor and others were defeated by the thick armor the creature wore, although his well-worn leather took scuffs and slices from the blades. Two penetrated, though—a heavy cleaver and a chef's knife. Her foe's eyes filled with pain and anger.

A hammering on the rear door distracted her for an instant, and the power needed to maintain the shields doubled as the enemy outside applied their magic to the task of breaking in. The giant in front of her moved the sword to the same hand as the ax, dragged the knife out, and hurled it at her, then repeated the process with the cleaver. She slapped them aside with a force shield and enjoyed the sight of his blood dripping on the floor.

He stabbed forward repeatedly with the spiked top of the larger weapon, which forced her to take a step back and block with each strike. Voices sounded behind him in shouts and snarls, and the realization that others might enter surged adrenaline and fear through her. She dropped the shield and attempted a force blast to thrust him back, but he weathered the blow easily. Frustrated, she tried ice. This failed to encase or harm him and she then tried fire, which caused him to pause his attack to protect his face but otherwise accomplished little.

The delay was as dangerous as the weapons he wielded. If the enemies outside broke in before help arrived, she would be all out of options. *"So, no more playing with the Kilomea. End him."* The voice was a strange amalgam of Nylotte, Fury, and the mental version of herself, but they were all correct. The stalemate couldn't continue. She dug deep for her magic and fired darts of flame—backed by as much power as she could pack into them—at his eyes. He raised a hand in time, but the wicked bolts burned through the hasty defense and he fell.

She had a moment to enjoy the success before Jarkko stepped through the door, an arrogant smirk on his face. "Oh, well done, Diana Sheen. I'd feared he would defeat you and deny me the pleasure of flaying the flesh from your bones." He carried an ornate dagger in his left hand, the blade a wicked serpentine creation of black metal and the hilt decorated with what looked like teeth. It was beyond gruesome.

"That's a nice knife. It suits you, little man."

He rolled his eyes contemptuously. "Short jokes. How original. At this decisive moment—the end of your existence—that's all you can come up with? It really is a pity."

The dwarf raised his free hand and a cone of shadow larger than any she'd ever seen expanded to cover her. Her defense wasn't fast enough or big enough to block the unexpected attack, and the power washed over her. As always, it filled her with darkness and made her choke on her own futility. But unlike in previous encounters, the dark magic didn't overwhelm her, not even momentarily. Barriers she didn't know she had snapped into place, constructed of confidence, experience, and the connections forged with others like her who fought against people like him. It took a few seconds for them to solidify before she shrugged the mental assault off and expanded her shield against the physical one.

Diana had expected the tentacles but was still annoyed by their appearance. She backpedaled to avoid them and yanked open the door of a large refrigerator to protect her from the shadow attacks. When she banished her magical defenses, she peeked around the barricade and used her telekinesis to slide a huge salad cooler into the doorway behind the dwarf. It would only delay his reinforcements for a short time but all she needed was thirty seconds. If she didn't eliminate him by then, her strength wouldn't be sufficient to both maintain the shield over the rear exit and continue to fight. In short, that would be the end.

"Come out of your hiding place, little human," he shouted. "It's time to die."

She shook her head and yelled, "Come and get me, coward." The heavy steel door rattled from the attacks he threw at it but remained strong. She flung a force bolt around the side to keep him occupied while she scanned the area for something to use to her advantage and finally discovered what she needed under a bread oven that stood tall beside her. Quickly, she kicked the metal tube and on the third blow, the pipe broke free. She pushed it into position with her foot and used her telekinesis to pull it until the opening pointed across the aisle. Satisfied, she backed away, swung the door partially closed with her magic, and raised her working arm.

"Okay, okay. I give up."

The angle was such that he couldn't see all of her and she gambled on the probability that he'd want to enjoy a clear view when he killed her. For a moment, it almost seemed that her hope was unfounded but her expectations were rewarded when he advanced, slammed the refriger-ator shut, and stopped almost where she wanted him.

This was the crunch. She put a whine in her voice and let the pain show. "Please, can we make an arrangement?"

He regarded her with a condescending sneer. "The only compromise is a quick death, human."

The agent gave a one-armed shrug. "Okay. No deal." She launched a fireball forward and dove to her left, over the top of the cooking counter. She landed painfully on her wounded arm as the ball of flame intersected the flow from the gas line she'd broken and erupted into a true conflagra-tion. The dwarf's scream was all she could have hoped for, and she stood painfully while he staggered and burned. She drew and hurled a throwing knife, pierced him in the chest, and tossed the other from her right boot into his shoulder for good measure. He fell and suddenly, the assaults on the doorways stopped.

The sound of sirens crept into the corner of her hearing as she swayed a little and tried to focus. She wondered belatedly where the wait staff had gone and checked the freezer in the back, fearing the worst. For the first time that evening, something didn't prove disastrous and she found them bound but mostly unharmed. She freed the captives with another of her knives and led the way out the rear door, which was now free of opposition.

Police and medical personnel appeared seemingly from nowhere to help everyone out to the arriving ambulances. She separated from the group and staggered toward her car, which always had two potions in the glove box for emergencies. She triggered her comm again. "This is Diana. Ambush at my location. EMTs on scene. I'm hurt."

The ensuing gabble of responses entered through one ear and failed to gain purchase before they exited via the other. Her focus was on the Mustang Fastback that held the answer to the throbbing agony in her arm. When she was ten feet away from it, she used the last of her magical energy to open the door, fearful that her physical strength might not be up to that simple task.

The explosion triggered by the movement of the handle was like a giant's fist had punched her squarely in the face, hurled her into the wall behind her, and pounded her head on the brick. She fell, vaguely aware of the feet of emergency personnel who raced in her direction, the last image she saw as her consciousness spun into darkness.

CHAPTER EIGHT

Kayleigh had rated her day as good and maybe even great until the news that the boss had been attacked had blown it to smithereens. She'd thrown her keyboard across the room, used her phone to summon a car, and dashed out of the house in a rage. The ride into town was spent coordinating the fallout from the ambush, ensuring that Tony and Hank were on the way to meet the ambulance, and informing Cara she was in charge until the hospital succumbed to Diana's complaints and released her.

She climbed out of the sedan a couple of blocks away for the sake of secrecy and jogged through the parking garage to the basement entrance. As soon as she entered, Deacon's voice sounded over her comm. "I see you're finally here. It took you long enough."

Annoyance flared at his attempt to lighten the mood and she pushed it aside. "No time for banter. What have you found out?" Her first notification about the situation had come from him since he'd been at the HQ working on who-knew-what while she was at home fighting noobs online and off-comms. She reached the staircase and ran up the steps to his lab.

He spun in his chair as she burst into their shared workspace. "I tracked her movements, but there was nothing interesting. So I accessed her phone. Bryant sent her a text inviting her to dinner. But it wasn't actually him. He's en route to join her, too, by the way."

With a brisk nod, she slid into the seat beside his. "Good. That'll make her happy. She's gonna be upset to be on the receiving end of the protocol she insisted on." Their boss had determined that any injury worthy of a healing potion had to be followed up by a trip to the hospital at the earliest opportunity, just in case. The field agents had all grumbled separately, tried to talk her out of it collectively, and finally agreed. Now, she would be the one stuck in bed.

"Yeah, karma's a bitch, right?" He spun to view his interfaces and called up an image of the text chat on the main screen. "So, here's what went down. It's enough like Bryant's style to suggest it wasn't simply a clumsy effort to pose as him. They must have had a look at how he writes somehow."

Kayleigh frowned. "So, they're in Bryant's system?"

Her colleague shrugged. "His. Ours. Both. There's no way to tell from this. But fortunately, I'm really good at what I do."

She groaned when he did things that caused the picture of the text to vanish and be replaced by a diagram. It contained innumerable boxes and lines and made no sense at all. He held his hands out as if she should understand,

and she blew out an exasperated breath. "Hey, rain man, not all of us are techno-savants. Do you care to explain?"

His chuckle eased something in her stomach. "Sure. I forget sometimes that you people are slow." Even though he was clearly kidding, the comment earned him a sharp punch on the shoulder. "Ow. Okay, look here." He pressed a button and several of the lines and boxes were outlined in yellow. "This one source has targeted our security for a while. The AIs blocked the attempts and it kept coming back but never registered as penetrating the outer firewall, so we didn't get an alert."

"Right. Got it. Is that relevant, or are you merely showing off?"

Deacon grinned. "A little of both. You know me too well." He pressed another button, and a set of frequencies appeared on a different screen. "I analyzed the timing of the attacks and compared them to the signals registered by the phones. It turns out there's a connection."

"If I wasn't aware of your dedication to privacy issues, I'd have to be concerned about your level of access to everyone's private lives."

He nodded. "Rightfully so. I read your emails for fun but that's really it." When she didn't rise to the bait, he pressed a few more buttons and the screen zoomed in. "The surveillance is all AI, as we agreed from the start. Even this analysis doesn't look strictly at content, only signals. But over half of these attacks on our security happened while this signal was present." He pointed at one that flashed red. "As it turns out, it's a GPS signature for a drone."

She started to ask how he was sure of that but shook

her head. *It doesn't matter and isn't worth getting him off track.* "And?"

"Do you know what drones are really good at? Visual surveillance."

Her jaw gaped in surprise. "Wait. You're telling me they stole his writing style, not by intercepts but using damn pictures taken by a drone?"

"Yep. You got it in one."

"Bloody hell." Her mind raced. "There's no easy way to prevent that?"

"We use electronic dampeners so the image doesn't go beyond the device and screens that block angled views, but with enough time, enough luck, and the right technology, it's doable. We can't guard against everything."

"Okay, we know how they knew how to impersonate him. How did they get the message onto her phone?"

Deacon sighed. "That's where we screwed up. It was preventable, but we didn't think of it." She motioned for him to continue. "Our phones are customized versions of commercial models because developing our own from scratch would be ridiculously complicated."

"Right."

"Unfortunately for us, the components are made in a country that has shown a significant interest in our activities."

"Shit. China."

He nodded. "The signal that arrived as a text also included additional data. It appears that allowed them to hijack Bryant's contact information at a level beneath where our security begins—something in the actual hard-ware. The bastards."

"So they've had access to all our stuff all along?"

Deacon shook his head. "No, we wouldn't have been able to find their fingerprints when we examined the oversight committee members if that was the case. I think this is a really specific thing that doesn't send data out, only accepts it. I'll have more to report once I have some hardware people from the CIA look into it. They were fairly upset when I reported it."

Kayleigh chuckled at the clear understatement. "I can only imagine. I bet they're ripping the phones out of the executive branch's hands right now." She shook her head. "How do we deal with this going forward?"

"The components for our comms and computers are all sourced from the United States and allied countries. We should default to those for any and all communication. The AIs can set up private connections to mimic our phones to make one-to-one conversations easy. I can't do much on the texting front, but emails and our secure computer app should be fine."

"Is there a way to turn this back on the bastards behind the attack?"

He raised an eyebrow. "From what I hear over the police channels, the boss took care of that personally—extra-crispy dwarf, I believe."

She paused, momentarily shocked, and burst into laughter. "Oh, my God, you're awful."

"You're too uptight, Kitana." He joined her mirth with a belly-laugh of his own.

With a sigh, she allowed herself to relax for the first time since she'd received the news. "Can we nail the people in Chinese Intelligence or whatever who are working with the Oricerans?"

Deacon yawned and stretched. "Not easily. It could be anyone in their government, really, and we have no way to narrow it down. We'll have to leave that part to the spies."

"What about the drones, though. Could we do something against those?"

"Now you're talking." He grinned. "I thought that one of our stun models should be able to mess up the electronics in anything other than hardened military UAVs. Do you want to go hunting?"

"Oh, hell yeah."

"Flight sticks and VR goggles are in there." He pointed at a cabinet on the far side of the room. "Grab a couple of each and let's see if we can destroy some high-priced Chinese technology."

Diana sat in her bed and growled her annoyance at the three men in front of her. "Listen, I'm fine. I need to get to headquarters and decide how to strike back at the bastards." The beeping of the EKG grated on her nerves, and it took all her restraint to not simply annihilate it with a bolt of electricity.

Tony laughed. "Now, boss, rules are rules."

Hank added, "Especially when they're your rules. I believe you said no exceptions, didn't you?"

The smugness in their tones made her want to bolt up and knock their heads together.

Bryant, seated on the bed beside her, patted her leg. "It's

okay. This is a good place for you to be while we determine if there'll be a follow-up attempt. The building's secure, no one knows you're here, and we have watchers all around."

She folded her arms and glared at the trio. "Get me an energy potion and I'll be great."

He twisted to look at the other two men. "You guys can head out and oversee the surveillance. Set up a replacement schedule so someone is on-site until she's released tomorrow." They waved and left, their grins showing relief that she would quickly be returned to full health and amusement that she was stuck in the bed against her will. He turned to reveal his own grin. "So, it looks like we have some quality time together."

"If you think I'll make out with you in this hospital, you have another think coming." She gave him a hard stare. "Get me an energy potion and take me to a hotel, and you'll find yourself well rewarded—very well rewarded." She imagined her flirting game was probably fairly weak at the moment, and his reaction confirmed it.

He tried and failed to stifle a laugh. "While that seems like a wonderful—and terrifying—invitation, I'll have to pass. We're in the same place at the same time and in a secure room. It's a perfect opportunity to talk more about Project Adonis."

CHAPTER NINE

Bryant stepped through the portal that connected Diana's home—where he'd now deposited her after her hospital stay—and Senator Finley's building. He hadn't slept much as he'd been awakened by every shift she'd made while sleeping and now had murder on his mind as he strode toward the neutral ground of the conference room. *No official office visit today, nothing that can be easily tracked.* He veiled himself in illusion to avoid attracting the attention of anyone he passed and carried a handy ARES device that would freeze camera feeds momentarily as he crossed their sightlines.

The senator was waiting when he arrived, two cups of coffee already on the table. Bryant took the closest one and dipped the finger with the flesh-colored chip into it surreptitiously as he raised it slowly to his lips. His comm made a gentle chime to indicate a lack of anything harmful, and he sipped the strong brew gratefully. Since the attack on Diana, maximum safety protocols were in effect, including checking beverages provided by allies for poison.

Finely didn't notice or if he did, chose not to remark on it. "Thanks for coming, Bryant. How's Sheen?"

He sighed and lowered the mug. "She's fine. Sleeping the potions off, for now. She'll be out for a while." In truth, she'd be unconscious for at least another day now that the after-effects of the healing had overwhelmed her stubborn resistance to sleep, but he didn't feel the need to share that information with anyone other than the Pittsburgh BAM agents.

The other man ran a hand through his perfectly trimmed brown hair with a nod. "Good. That's good. I'm afraid everything I have to offer today is bad." Bryant sipped again and waited. Finley's voice communicated his discomfort. "The committee is now back to full strength. I've delayed convening it because you all are 'fully occupied with tactical operations' at the moment, but that ploy won't last for long."

"What's the damage?"

Finley stood suddenly and began to pace. He had never seen the man so agitated. *This doesn't bode well.* "The two the vice president added are both hawks and much more interested in overt action than covert action because it plays better to the media and their constituents. While they might not agree with Cyphret all the time, they'll be of like mind with her more often than not." He sat again and put his palms flat on the table. "Honestly, I think the VP may have chosen them to force a vote to disband ARES. And I'm not sure, given the way the organization has been compromised, that I can stop it."

Bryant shook his head and heat surged through him.

"Yeah, compromised thanks to that very committee. That's damn thin, Aaron."

"I know, I know." He threw his hands up in frustration. "And I can't do a thing about it. I'm solidly outranked on this one, obviously." He lowered them again and leaned back in his chair. "Seriously, I am at a loss like I've never been before on this project. Every way I look, we're screwed."

"I hear that. My people are working on options in that area, as you are well aware." He wouldn't mention Adonis openly, even with the signal jammer in his pocket. "What can I do to help you stall them?"

The senator sighed. "The best choice might be to stay unreachable. Keep anyone from locating you if possible. I'll keep saying you're deep in operations and off the grid. That won't stop them from meeting and taking action in your absence, but I have to think that will be a last option rather than their first move."

"You don't sound sure of that."

"I'm not. These people are serious manipulators with a wealth of experience, and they're in the VP's pocket. Or maybe it's the other way around. Either scenario is not good. Very not good."

"I hear you, Senator."

"I'd watch out for sudden visits from other agencies, too. There's no telling what these bastards will do."

He raised an eyebrow. "Okay. We'll go with your plan to delay and lock down the known facilities. Is there any chance you'll be able to give us a warning if they make a move?" The look on Finley's face told the story without the need for words. He was a man who'd been cut off at the knees and his authority in this particular area had vanished like it had never existed. Bryant sighed. "Gotcha." He rose and extended a hand.

His counterpart stood and gripped it. "I'll do all I can, but we both know that won't be enough. It's been a pleasure knowing you, Special Agent in Charge Bates."

"You as well, Senator Finley. You've been a good friend to ARES, and I've always appreciated it. Don't go too far out on that ledge for us. We've got this."

He laughed. "Let the professionals handle it, is that what you're saying?"

"More or less." Bryant grinned. "You are the expert on your playing field, but these bastards seem to want to walk onto mine. They don't realize how different the rules are. But if they step over the line, they'll definitely find out." He released the other man's hand.

Finley nodded. "Take care."

"You too." He waited as the senator left the room and headed to his next task. Bryant remained for a moment and planted the listening devices Emerson had designed, which were undetectable except by sight or touch. They hijacked the personal technologies of anyone in proximity to send their signals and made it impossible to separate the ARES information from whatever the person was doing with their phone or tablet. It wouldn't be sent in real-time as they used burst transmissions, but it would be close enough that they'd have a warning.

That done, he walked to the hole in the building's anti-magic defenses and portaled to the ARES DC base. There were people to put under surveillance and contingency plans to activate, and he had absolutely no time to waste.

CHAPTER TEN

Hank slammed the door of the black SUV a little harder than strictly necessary. *If one of the ambushing bastards was here tonight, that would make this extra special.* He needed to blow off steam, and there was only a single thing that worked for that. The anticipatory look on Cara's face as she rounded the front of the car to join him showed that she felt the same. They were both overdue for a fight.

The warehouse was filled to the brim, more crowded than he'd ever seen it. She waved as she pushed into the crowd to renew acquaintances and seek a bout, and he headed toward the club's overseer. The man was engrossed in conversation with two people who had the look of newcomers and he doubtless explained that this was not a place for tourists, only for those ready to throw down with everything they had. He looked up and smiled at the agent's approach, his unnaturally white teeth sparkling in the mess that was his fully out-of-control mustache and beard. His long, dark, scraggly hair was bound in a ponytail that reached the middle of his black denim jacket. Dirty blue jeans and paint-splashed work boots completed the look.

He spoke in a boisterous voice that carried easily above the surrounding hubbub. "H, good to see you again!" True names were generally withheld at the events—or at the very least not shouted. He shooed away the two he'd been entertaining and strode forward with a paw extended.

"What are you up to, Kev?" Hank shook it with a wry smile. While researching the man as part of his due diligence on the club before he'd joined, he'd discovered his name was actually Stanley. Despite his frequent telling of the story of his immigration from Ukraine, he had been born in Detroit. *Whatever. No one comes here to find any truth other than the kind delivered by fists and feet.*

"Same old, same old, brah. You?"

"Exactly."

Kev laughed. "How many are you looking for tonight?" Newcomers often mistook the question, as bouts with more than two people weren't allowed.

"Single. But a good one. Do you know anyone?"

His ponytail swayed with the nod of his head. "Yeah. I have a couple of regulars, plus a newcomer. He's hard—at your nine o'clock, halfway up the bleachers."

The agent swiveled to the right first, then to the left and feigned disinterest. The unfamiliar face in question was immediately apparent and the man towered at least a half-foot taller than those around him. Huge muscles bulged in his arms and chest, and his neck looked like it could support a skyscraper balanced on his skull. "Holy hell."

The organizer laughed again with a note of disbelief in

it. "Right? He's a specimen, to be sure. 'Roid rager is my guess."

"Or maybe part-Kilomea."

The other man raised his palms and shook his head. "I did not need that picture. You can't unimagine a thing like that. Thanks, dude." He lowered his hands. "Anyway, he introduced himself and said he was looking for the toughest guy around. That's usually you. Are you interested?"

That's quite a coincidence. Either way, it's worth further investigation. "Yeah, set it up."

With a nod, the man in charge tapped his phone. "Okay, I can make some lesser bouts wait. Is fifteen minutes good?"

"Perfect. I'll go warm up." He crossed to the portion of the warehouse he favored for preparation and moved through a series of full-body routines to ready his muscles efficiently for the battle to come. His magic stirred in anticipation and he pushed it down. One day, it would be fun to have a magically enabled bout, but it wouldn't be fair among these people who lacked his arcane advantages.

The minutes passed quickly, and he headed to the ring to wait for the current match to end. Partway there, Cara intercepted him with another woman at her side. Her companion had bright purple hair cut into a short spiky style. He nodded, and she returned the gesture. "Brin."

"Hank."

His fellow-agent looked around to make sure no one paid attention to them. "She has information you need to hear."

He raised an eyebrow and his new acquaintance said, "Your fight is a setup."

"Excuse me?"

The other woman sighed as Brin launched into her explanation. "So, the dude you're paired with has been here for several nights. He fought but I've watched him, and he always seemed like he was waiting for something. When you two walked in, he perked right the hell up."

So, you were watching for us too. Or maybe Cara. He grinned at the idea. *They'd make a cute couple, although Anik would probably have an objection, knowing him.* "Kev said he's a newcomer."

Cara snorted. "Kev's a lying asshole who doesn't care about anything other than his side action." Even though betting was strictly disallowed, the rules didn't apply to the organizer and his circle of intimates. "We should get out of here now."

Hank shook his head. "No chance. There are two options if Brin is right. First, he's heard about me here and wants to mix it up. That's nothing to worry about. Second, it's something like what happened to you and Diana, in which case, he can explain the situation when he's bleeding on the floor."

"It's an unnecessary risk."

He grinned. "Are you gonna order me not to?"

She sighed. "No. If you have to be an idiot, go be an idiot. We'll be nearby on the off chance that you want an assist. Do you have a potion?"

"In my bag."

"We'll bring it. A big chucklehead like you might need two."

The current match ended with a chorus of cheers and boos, and he pushed through the standing crowd to enter the rectangular fighting area. His opponent was the promised hulking brute, who loomed a head above even Hank. *Hell, he didn't look that big sitting down.* The man's muscles rippled, and his bald scalp shone in the lights from above. His face told his history, his nose and at least one cheekbone broken and poorly set at some time in the past. He seemed to be aware of the effect his looks had on others because he grinned to display several cracked teeth when he caught his opponent's stare.

They walked slowly to the center of the ring. Neither wanted to be the first one there and give the appearance of waiting for the other. Both men wore the same outfits in identical shades—black boots, blue jeans, and white tank t-shirts. They shook under Kev's watchful gaze when the overseer appeared out of the crowd to join them with a happy grin on his face.

Clearly, he has a little action going. I wonder who he's betting on. Up close, his opponent was absolutely huge, bigger even than a Kilomea. *Truly a specimen and definitely chemically boosted. This could be a little challenging.*

The beast growled before he spoke. "You're Hank. I'm Gregori. You're about to...lose." The pause was notable, and he was about to ask about it when he was interrupted by the third man in the middle of the ring.

"Okay, you know the deal. Everything's fair. Unless you want to choose the house rules?" The two men stared at each other and neither responded. "Good. The fight ends when one can't go on anymore or when one surrenders. We'll stop you every couple of minutes for a reset." He leaned in and spoke barely loud enough to be heard. "Be sure not to break anything other than each other, huh, guys?" After a grin, he threw his hands up and yelled, "Corners." Hank retreated to the right and the other man jogged to the opposite end of the ring.

"Fight!" Kev's shout was accompanied by a raucous cheer from the crowd and the agent strode toward the middle to meet the larger man, who matched his movement. Hank had fought big men before—although not this huge—and had found they shared a common weakness. The muscle significantly hindered their mobility. It was one of the reasons he included Yoga and Tai Chi in his own training routine. He feinted with his left and threw a slow right hook to test the waters.

Gregori's block jarred his arm with the force of a punch, far stronger than he'd expected even given the man's size. His foe tried to use the block to slip in a straight punch to his face, but the agent skipped back and defocused his eyes so he could see all of his opponent at once. *Dammit. That hurt.* The colossus moved like a much smaller person and negated the edge he'd hoped to have. Hank took two quick steps forward and launched a kick at his adversary's groin with his left foot. When the man shifted to block it, he vaulted off his back foot and pistoned it at the broad chest. It struck and drove his target back at least a few inches.

He rubbed his pecs and grinned. "That was a good shot. But if this is all you have, the battle will not go well for you."

Shit. "Less talking, more fighting, Sasquatch."

In response, the hulk bared his teeth and waded in, a

wave of elbows and knees that immediately put his rival on the defensive. The aggressor was deceptively quick, and each time Hank thought he had a window to counterattack, his foe blocked it before he'd even thrown the punch. *It's like he can read my mind.* The realization struck him between the eyes as hard as a blow and distracted, he overlooked the actual fist that pounded into his forehead. He stumbled away, instantly dizzy, and fell. As he prepared himself to catch the kick that was no doubt on its way, the horn sounded to signal the end of the round.

Strong arms helped him up. Cara and Brin each took a side and dragged him, stumbling, into his corner. His coworker's voice was filled with worry. "What happened?"

The agent blinked against the stars that swarmed in his vision. "He's cheating. I'm sure he has a mind reader or something. There's no other explanation. No one's that good."

She frowned. "We should bail. This is way too much of a coincidence." Brin looked from one to the other, confusion on her face. Cara sighed and explained, "It would take too long for the whole story. Let's simply say there are bad people after us and they use magic."

The other woman's eyes widened. "What she said. You should run."

Hank laughed. "He's not the only one with powers. And if he's not following the rules, that means I don't have to, either." He palmed the healing potion Cara held out to him, drank half of it, and returned it without anyone noticing. The draught burned through him to clear both his vision and his thoughts. He stood and rolled his neck. "Okay, I'll kick his ass. Afterward, though, be ready to run."

The women nodded, and as he walked to the center, he heard Cara trying to convince Brin to leave. *Great idea but she's probably dumb, exactly like us.* He grinned. *I wanted a good fight, so I might as well quit worrying and enjoy it now that I have one.*

His opponent looked confident, doubtless believing he had Hank's measure. His accent sounded like some kind of guttural version of Russian. "Are you sure you wouldn't like to surrender and avoid pain?"

He merely cracked his knuckles and stretched his arms wide. "Are you sure you wouldn't like to?"

The other man answered with an abrupt charge and abandoned the up-close attacks for a martial art that focused on sharp, fast moves. The agent remained loose and blocked and evaded while each contact fueled the magical energy pool inside him. Gregori landed a couple of solid punches to his body and while they hurt, they didn't hit anything fragile. He'd have bruises worth talking about but no broken bones.

When he could feel the power ooze into each drop of sweat that fell, he moved into the attack. He waited for one of the other man's punches and channeled his magic into speed. His arm lashed out and his fist impacted his foe's chest with enough force to make him stumble. He grinned. "What's the matter, friend? Have you lost your edge?" It was as close as he could get to mentioning the magic without causing a scene that might put everyone else in danger. If the other fighters knew they actually used powers, the trust that made the club work would collapse. *And, dammit, I need this place.*

His opponent looked like he was thinking hard—or maybe it was simply that any and all thought was hard for him. Either way, a look of concern crept into his eyes, and the agent was satisfied to have put it there. He grew tired of waiting for a reply and danced to defend several times while he waited for an opportunity. The other man swung a frustrated hook that left him open, and he dodged in, intercepted the blow with the opposite hand, and spun to face away from his opponent and hurl a back fist. Gregori ducked sufficiently to take it on the forehead, but it left him a little dazed. Hank stepped forward, kicked back with his full strength, and added magic for speed and power. His heel thumped into the man's pelvis and splintered the bone with a resounding crack.

The giant howled and stumbled one step before he collapsed. He knelt quickly beside him. "Do you yield?"

Gregori snarled and punched at his head but he caught the arm, locked it, and shattered the elbow with a hammer fist. He twisted the injured joint as he leaned down to speak into the man's ear. "I know you're magical. I know you intended to kill me because why else would you do this? Is there more to the plan?"

His opponent maintained his silence until he dislocated the shoulder attached to the man's wounded arm with a sharp blow. Tears welled from his eyes as he forced the words out. "Ambush...after...for the girl."

The agent stood with a sigh, calculated the right amount of force, and applied the toe of his boot to Gregori's temple. Cheers erupted among the onlookers. He stalked out of the combat area to find Cara and discovered her near the exit. "There's an ambush waiting. He was supposed to eliminate me—as if you need me to beat these stupid assholes."

She slapped him on the arm. "That's why I like you, Hank. You always recognize my innate superiority." She laughed and he joined in. Brin stood nearby, and they strode over to her. Cara sounded sheepish or embarrassed. "I'm afraid the people we mentioned have traced us here, which means you might be in danger if you walk out since you've been seen with us. You'll have to come with us but we'll get you home."

To her credit, the woman didn't argue and merely walked with them to a darkened corner of the warehouse where the ARES second in command summoned a portal. They strode through and vanished from sight. Before he followed, Hank considered that the smart move would probably be to go back and kill the giant. *Hey, but no one ever accused me of being smart.* He put the worry aside and stepped through to safety.

CHAPTER ELEVEN

Deacon deposited the haul from the convenience store on the table behind his desk. Only the AIs were there to hear him mutter, "All right, all right, all right," as he separated the items. A twelve-pack of Coke went on one side, Spicy Chili Doritos on the other, and in the center, he placed a box of the almost-plastic tiny chocolate donuts that were his particular vice.

He crunched a few chips, popped the top on a can, and drank half of it in a long series of gulps. With a satisfied sigh, he plunked it down and sat in his high-backed computer chair. Doing his most important tasks late at night or in the early morning hours had begun as a means to avoid sharing bandwidth or processing power. Now, it was merely a habit, but he had to admit there was something special about the dark and quiet building when he was the only person around.

Yeah, it's a great setup for a murder scene in a horror film. Let's get to it. His fingers danced, and he issued verbal commands to bring his tools online and uncouple his rig from the internal network. One of the first things he'd done upon arrival was to have a diverter inserted in the building's main link to the Internet and a backup installed. Anyone renting space and unlucky enough to be in as early as he was would find themselves limited to average wireless speed as the fiber connection to the outside now only fed his machines—in part for speed but mainly for security.

When his equipment was isolated, he summoned his magic and slipped into the virtual world it provided. His body would continue to issue commands through his mouth and fingers to bring his avatar's actions to life in code, but he wouldn't be aware of it. From his perspective, the electronic dragon he was out to slay had become a real one.

A castle loomed before him across an expanse of flat grass meant to deny an attacker cover. It was made of red stone, and each of the four corner towers and the main keep featured pagoda-like pointed and curved protrusions decorating each level. They shone with gold in the sunlight. The moat that surrounded it was as wide as a river and glistened with sparkles and leaping fish in rainbow hues. Guards in ebony armor marched atop the crenelated walls, holding tall pikes that flashed every so often as they reflected the overhead brilliance.

The dragon in question appeared to be asleep, its sinuous body wound around the top of the keep's tallest tower on a ledge that had no doubt been built for that specific purpose. It was gold and black, with crimson accents that matched the blocks perfectly.

I certainly didn't think it would be easy, but this is a little more challenging than I'd expected. In the real world, he looked at the firewalls and protective programs that defended the home of the people who'd messed with ARES. It had taken considerable research to definitively connect the oversight committee surveillance to the attack on Diana, and despite telling Kayleigh it was impossible, he'd managed it. Unlike most of his statements of that nature—which were essentially to emphasize his brilliance when he actually achieved the act in question—he'd meant it about the Chinese. But they'd left the tiniest thread unclipped and he had tugged on it until it led him there. *Which, of course, could always be a trap.*

His avatar was a character he'd once played in a video game. It was short, thin, and clad in heavily oiled and virtually silent black leather armor. His boots were the same—well-worn and unlikely to betray his presence. A fabric mask that matched the outfit covered his face except for a narrow band across the eyes. His visible skin was charcoaled. *Perfect for a night assault, but it's apparently always day here.* He shrugged and indulged a wish for the interior to be dark when he finally arrived inside.

He reached for cloaking programs and shrouded his avatar in illusion. First, he made the armor vanish, which left him naked. Second, he modified his features and tailored them to the setting. His hair lengthened and bound itself into a topknot. A long, thin mustache grew and the ends drooped several inches below his jaw. The garb of a merchant appeared, the colorful tunic and pants designed to draw notice rather than avoid it. The final touch was a cart full of tools and cunning clockwork toys, with clanging pots and pans on a suspended pole. *Simply your ordinary everyday tinker come to call. Is the dragon available for a chat?*

Deacon snorted as he shoved the wagon along the long, winding road that led to the castle. There was a tradesman's gate to one side of the main one, little more than a door wide enough to accommodate his cart, and he angled in that direction. The path ended at the moat, and he called out, "Tinker Chaoxiang, toys and repairs." In the real world, his invasion programs pushed at weaknesses they'd identified during the time his avatar walked toward the structure.

One of the guards bristled and told him to go away, but another asked, "What kinds of toys?" He smiled and held up a cunningly crafted bird that hovered above his hand. Its mechanical wings beat furiously as the spring inside unwound. It landed, and the man laughed in delight. "Most wonderful! Open the small gate."

Ahead, the barrier opened and a stone bridge rose dripping from beneath the waves to allow passage across the water. He resumed pushing his cart and crossed into his enemy's stronghold.

It had taken an apparent eternity of pretense to work his way through the guards and servants milling about the grounds outside the keep to finally gain entry. It was notably less bright with windows abandoned in favor of security and only burning oil lamps to provide illumination. He pushed his cart into a forgotten corner and melted into the shadows, abandoned his illusion, and summoned his dark armor. The tower with the dragon was his goal. He didn't need to kill the creature—in fact, he would prefer to avoid it—but all signs pointed to the secrets he'd come to claim resting at the top of the pinnacle.

A spiral staircase climbed the wide structure in sections. Each graceful curve ended at a potentially occupied area and resumed on the opposite side. Sneaking past was his first choice, but as he approached the second level and extended a small periscope, it was apparent that he wouldn't be that fortunate. Two guards sat on low stools in the middle of the room with their helmets on the floor near their feet. They laughed and joked with a serving girl, whose back was to him.

Dammit. But at least their hats are off. He retrieved the blow darts secured at his waist. He carried five, that being one of his lucky numbers, and another five of the slender needles balanced and feathered for throwing rested beside them. Each was coated in a potent sleep potion that would take effect almost instantly and last for approximately an hour on a person of average build.

He raised three to his mouth, made sure the spread was correct, and angled the one in the middle up slightly. A deep breath in through his nose was the preamble to an explosive exhale through the tubes, and the missiles sped true. The guard on the left was struck in the cheek, the servant on the back of the neck, and the guard on the right in the forehead, which was the only part of him visible around the object of their attention.

The trio fell, the woman in silence and the men with a soft clatter as the metal studs on their leather armor impacted the floor. He crept forward and searched them for keys but found none. With a quiet curse, he arranged them as if they were sleeping, mainly because he had no time to come up with a better solution. From the moment he'd entered the castle, the clock on the operation had been ticking.

Deacon darted to the next level and was taken by surprise when a sentry stepped into his path. He launched at him with an acrobatic tumble, wound his legs around the man's neck, and used his body weight to flip his opponent as gravity pulled him down. The man fell heavily and succumbed to a dagger thrust under his chin before he could recover from the shock of the maneuver. The hacker congratulated himself internally before a piercing pain radiated from his side. He twisted and felt for a knife that protruded from his lower back, yanked it out as he spun, and threw it at another guard who had attacked.

His new opponent batted it aside with his free hand and swung his longsword at the intruder's head. The slightly curved blade loomed large in Deacon's vision as it approached. He flipped away from the attack and it caught only his hair and severed an inch at the end. When his feet touched the floor, he vaulted again, this time in a flying kick at his adversary.

The man brought his sword up in defense, but he knocked it away with one boot and planted the other in his foe's face. He kicked the stumbling man as he landed, a front strike to the solar plexus that was strong enough to double him over, even through the armor. He spun to the side and away from his enemy's sword hand and whipped a reverse hook kick with all the speed and momentum he could muster. His heel connected with the guard's temple and the man's eyes rolled back as he crumpled.

Deacon cast about for more enemies, but the remainder of the level was bare. The wound was painful but didn't hinder his movement. On the floor above, he encountered another servant, thankfully alone this time. He waved his hand and intoned, "I am not the intruder you're looking for," and the young man nodded once and continued to perform his duties. *They are much dumber than the guard programs. I wish the Jedi mind trick worked on them.*

The next floor up was vacant, as was the one after that. Although the interior of the tower bore no resemblance whatsoever to the view he'd had from the outside, he sensed that he was close to the pinnacle. He pressed himself against the wall of the stairs as he climbed and rotated his perspective methodically from left to right and back again to safeguard against surprises.

Still, when he stepped onto the next circular floor, etched glass walls fell to prevent him from either going higher or retreating. It was outfitted as a living room, with a roaring fire at the westerly compass point and curved bookshelves filling the remaining space. Two couches positioned at a right-angle basked in the heat from the flames, and two reading chairs stood beside one another across the room from them. The being materialized as unexpectedly as the barriers had, dressed exactly as he was but in white. He raised his gloved hands and offered a slow clap. "Well done. No one has penetrated our security so effectively in some time."

Shit. It's a person, not a program. Although AIs could mimic humans with increasing efficacy, he retained confidence in his ability to tell them apart. He hooked his thumbs into his weapons belt with a nod. "Your defenses are fairly strong, but you've failed to notice a hole or two."

A grin stretched the fabric of the pale mask. "If it pleases you to believe you found weaknesses, by all means, do so."

Deacon shook his head. "Typical bravado. Unwilling to admit your mistakes. I bet you work for the government in an ugly cubicle with neck strain from wearing your VR goggles fourteen hours a day." The other avatar stilled, which told him he'd scored a point. It recovered quickly, though, and gestured at the chamber around them.

"You are welcome to have a seat and wait. You won't be able to leave this room as we've hijacked your signal. It will be only a matter of time until you're reverse-traced to your rat hole, vermin."

"Yeah, right. I'm bouncing off so many proxies that you'll never find your way to me."

The other man nodded. "Again, believe so if you wish."

"Maybe I'll simply destroy you, instead, and be on my way." His opponent's threat was bravado as the physical kill switch near his body's feet could detach him from the virtual castle at any time. But he'd come there to achieve a specific goal and wasn't willing to leave without accomplishing it. *Unless they do find out how to track me, which would be bad.*

In the real world, his body and voice brought additional defensive programs online to guard against the enemy backtracking his trail. Immediately, the signal split and split again to spread false echoes exponentially across the Internet. His bandwidth and processor cycles for the assault would suffer, but it was all part of the game.

He surged toward the other man, who quickly broke to his left, away from the fire and the furniture. To counter this, he changed the angle and launched a roundhouse kick that was summarily blocked. His foe chopped at his neck with the hand that had stopped his leg, and he took the low-power shot on a lowered jaw. His opposite side fist lashed a punch at his opponent's solar plexus but it, too, was easily arrested. Counterattacks followed—kicks and punches in typical short, sharp karate style—and he was forced to disengage and retreat.

The man in white reached over his shoulder, drew a longsword, and lifted it to high attack position before he raced at him with a battle cry. The tech summoned his weapons, dual tonfa that were far more capable than the police nightstick version of the weapon. His were made of reinforced steel and the one along his left forearm clanged when it intercepted the downward chop of his opponent's blade. His other spun out as he twirled it in his grip and smacked into the other man's left thigh, hammered the nerve cluster, and dropped him to one knee. His follow-up strikes were blocked by clever twists of the sword, and his foe regained his feet and lurched forward, leading with the blade.

Deacon leapt over the couch to gain a little distance. His opponent followed and advanced slowly after his own jump carried him over the barrier. The white warrior used the length of his sword to defeat the invader's attacks before they started. A ticking clock suddenly echoed in his head to remind him he was running out of time.

Damn, their tracers must be top-shelf. He feigned an ankle twist and lurched to the side, and his foe seized the moment to charge, struck him with a front kick, and shifted his weight to bring the blade down. In the middle of the adjustment, when the other man's balance was at its most vulnerable, he threw the powder he'd palmed from his belt—coarse sand that would hurt the white warrior's vision more with each blink.

His adversary attempted a couple more slashes as he backed away but it was clear that he had lost the ability to see. Deacon circled quietly and launched a sidekick that thrust the man into the fire. His form brightened and vanished as the other hacker's systems succumbed to the attacks he'd directed at it. The glass barriers fell, a roar sounded from above, and he responded with a curse. He abandoned subtlety and raced up the stairs to find the dragon present on the inside of the tower on the top floor, the space far larger than it should be.

He dropped and slid to avoid the burst of flame his new and significantly larger opponent directed at him. His vision of a valiant battle vanished when the huge lizard reared on its back feet and towered above him. A glint of light on gold from the creature's horde behind its tail caught his eye, and he darted between its legs. He clambered up the sliding hill of coins as the beast roared again and twisted to locate him. The dragon drew in a breath and Deacon jumped and extended his arms as far as he could, and his fingers closed on the enormous diamond near the top. As the flames washed over him, his body kicked the switch and cast him out of the illusory realm.

It took a long moment for his heart rate to settle. He

sank into his chair and wiped his sweaty brow before he twisted to snag a handful of donuts. Once he'd polished two of them off, he took a drink of his coke and spat it out. *Flat, dammit.* With a shrug, he took another can and drained it completely. The sugar flowed into his system and stabilized him. Finally, he spun back and pressed the keys to bring up the data he'd stolen. *This had better be worth it.*

CHAPTER TWELVE

A day of peace and another of quiet had done wonders for Diana's attitude. She'd woken at home after the hospital, filled with anger at herself, anger at her enemies, and anger at the world in general. The result of that was that she'd gone directly to the security agency and worked herself to exhaustion with Fury. The sword seemed to understand what she needed and provided a steady flow of multiple opponents to challenge her. She hadn't stopped until she ran out of strength to hold the blade any longer and had slept on the hard floor for an hour before she summoned the energy to portal home to her own bed.

Now, though, her mood was fantastic. Deacon's hacking run had netted useful intel, things progressed on other fronts as they needed to, and the promise of information sharing with the kemana let her believe that any new problems would be detected before she wound up fighting for her life in a restaurant. She pushed open the door that led into the backyard with a cold bottle of beer in her hand.

Rath dashed past laughing, Max barking furiously at his heels. When they reached the grass, the dog leapt and tackled the troll, and they rolled in pretend fighting. Bryant looked up from where he preheated the huge grill they'd rented for the day and honestly looked beyond silly —and really cute—in the oversized chef's hat he'd adopted for the task. "Hey, you two, don't knock anything over."

The troll looked up, gave him a comical glare, and executed a jump and flip onto the middle of the long picnic table. He landed on the checkered tablecloth with his feet on either side of a large bowl of potato salad and another of macaroni salad. Bryant growled, and Rath flipped off the table again with a longer, louder laugh. He raced to the back of the yard where he'd put a knife-throwing lane along the long, high fence. The target was a cartoonish clown they'd found at a party store. She thought it was a little dark but he'd merely grinned and replied, "Dark is good. I like dark." Diana had more or less given up on trying to stop him from doing anything, content to simply try to nudge him to safer options.

She sidled up beside Bryant and kissed him on the cheekbone, standing on her toes to reach it. "Is the shield doing okay?" They had raised a protective barrier together that surrounded the backyard.

"Yep. As is the grill. As is the food that's being delivered. As is the stuff on the table. Chill out, woman."

"Anyone else who spoke to me like that would get a punch to the skull for their troubles." She smacked him gently on the back of the head.

He grinned. "You love it."

Diana shook her head and started to reply but the doorbell stopped her. She went into the house while Rath and Max pushed through at the same time to try to trip her, apparently, and opened the door. Hank stood on the threshold with Cara behind him. Each held a case of assorted brews from one of her favorite microbreweries. "Okay, you brought good beer so you're allowed to come in."

She led them out the back, and they veered toward the ice-filled coolers on the opposite side of the yard from the grill. The doorbell rang repeatedly, and she let people in one after the next until the whole team was present. When the last one arrived, the troll darted into the basement to separate Kayleigh and Deacon from their computer game, and the two cringed visibly from the light as they walked out into the warm late afternoon.

When they had all gathered, their boss stood on one of the benches and called for quiet. The individual conversations died down and she ordered them all to get drinks and waited while they did so. She raised her beer.

"To the best team anyone could ask for. No matter what they throw at us, we will always come back punching harder than they ever imagined. To you!" There was a chorus of echoes and some laughter, and she grinned at them. "We have a sight and sound shield up to block the backyard. No gunfire please, and those with magic among you, keep it in your pants, okay?" More laughter followed. "Otherwise, Rath is running the knife-throwing competition, Bryant has the beanbags for the cornhole tournament, and I'll wander around being the hostess of your nightmares. You're all welcome to crash here after, so for this one afternoon and evening, let your worries go and have fun."

She hopped down and Bryant gave her a nod of approval. Her seniority let her bull her way to the front of the line against Rath, and she lost miserably. She was reasonably sure he'd closed his eyes on the last throw, but his innocent look denied her confirmation. Cara was his next challenger and had already confided that Angel and Demon had given her tips. Diana leaned against the fence behind the throwers to watch the troll get trounced but was pulled away by Hank's hand on her arm.

The big man looked apologetic. "I'm sorry to delay the fun, boss, but I need to talk a little shop."

Diana finished her beer and arced the bottle into the large recycling bin. Max, who wore saddlebags filled with ice and beer, ran over in response to her whistle. The large man laughed as she took her new drink and she smiled at him. "Whatever makes you happy, that's the rule. If work stuff is blocking your enjoyment, let's get that junk taken care of."

He nodded and tilted his head before he moved into an unpopulated corner of the yard. She followed and stood across from him. He pitched his voice low. "So, I sense we may have to put the truck to use sooner rather than later with what's been going on."

She'd guessed that the various things they'd asked for—especially the AI backups on board—would give him an inkling of the larger picture. Optimistically, she'd hoped it would take longer because she didn't want to spook the team prematurely. She matched his tone. "A definite possibility, but not—and I can't stress this enough since I know how gossipy you and Cara are when you're together—not a certainty."

Hank managed to maintain his stern glare for almost six whole seconds before he broke into laughter. "All right, fair enough. But seriously, is there anything I should do to get ready for whatever's probably not going to happen?"

With a sigh, she said, "Simply be prepared to move on a moment's notice. Ideally, we won't have to go but if we do, it'll need to be fast."

"Go where?"

"That's enough, you." She punched him in the shoulder. "Get your ass back to the party."

Almost like they'd choreographed it, he was replaced by Tony. The detective had trimmed down and put muscle on by working with the other agents and glowed with health. His mustache had grown as well, and he resembled a gunslinger from the old west more and more each day. He grinned. "I have a complaint."

Diana shook her head. "I need a drink for this." She tipped the bottle and swallowed half of it before she returned her attention to him. "Honestly, when don't you have a complaint?"

He made a show of looking thoughtful, then shrugged. "Okay, maybe never. But that doesn't change the fact that I have one now."

"And it is?"

"Your boyfriend over there seems confused about how to cook a steak. He's taking orders that do not include the word 'rare.' It's a damn travesty."

She scowled as hard as she could. "This is a fucking emergency and no doubt about it. Lead on, Detective." She followed him to the grill and drained her drink on the way. The light feeling in her head permitted her to relax in a way other than forcing herself to exhaustion for the first time since the ambush. She punched Bryant in the shoulder blade.

He turned with an annoyed, "Ow," saw it was her, and grinned. "Oh, okay. You're allowed to hit me."

"Don't you forget it." She gestured at the grill. "There's been a report that you're mangling the steaks. Is this true?"

"Listen. It's not my fault that Deacon is uncivilized enough to want his steak medium." He glared accusingly over her head at Tony. "I'm merely here to serve."

The conflict over the steak promised to be epic as Tony departed in search of their hacker and she shook her head and crossed to the cooler. She took another drink, this one a single IPA, and gave Max a few belly rubs as a reward for his good work. There was a commotion from the picnic table and she noticed a crowd had gathered. She stood and wandered over slowly, half interested and half afraid of what she might find. The sight that greeted her was completely unexpected.

On one side of the table, Hank sat with his sleeve rolled up and his elbow on the surface in a classic arm-wrestling pose. On the other side, the seven-foot-tall purple-haired troll imitated his position. When she arrived, they clasped hands and grinned at one another. Cara shouted, "Go!" and the struggle commenced.

She assumed Rath would win, but Hank held his own. Their grins faded as they fought, and she saw sweat break out on the human's forehead. The troll made a strange keening sound as if he were building his power up with the rising tone of his voice. Their arms trembled. Finally, with a convulsive move, he slammed the human's hand down and bottles of ketchup and mustard scattered.

"And the troll wins!" she yelled, There was much laughter as the two shook hands and Hank rubbed his arm noticeably. The night continued at a casual pace. Large groups broke into small groups and came together again, everyone very much at ease with one another. It was exactly what she'd hoped for from the event—a chance for them all to connect someplace other than the office or the battlefield. Kayleigh and Deacon were the last to succumb to the need for rest—or maybe for gaming—and they headed down to the basement together.

Finally, it was only her and Bryant, not including the exhausted dog in the living room with the ten-inch troll curled in his fur. The sight brought a smile to her lips, and Bryant's hug from behind made everything right. She whispered, "This was perfect."

He kissed the back of her head. "Yep, it truly was a good plan. Who would have imagined the brash FBI agent I met so long ago would have such leadership qualities?"

Diana turned in his arms and stared into his eyes. "Do you know how close you are to death right now?"

"I was betrayed by my mouth," he protested with a grin.

She grinned at the reference, delivered in a rasp to acknowledge Kathleen Turner, and shook her head. "Then maybe you should do something more useful with it." She pulled him down into a kiss, and that was perfect, too.

CHAPTER THIRTEEN

Late the next morning, Diana slipped out of bed, careful not to wake Bryant. The headache that lingered around the corners of her brain was nothing more than a slightly off-key note in the positive music left by the party the day before. She showered and dressed in silence and donned her standard Kemana-visiting uniform of jeans and a concert t-shirt. Today's selection was Green Day, and "Peacemaker" played on repeat in her mind as she summoned a portal to the basement of Nylotte's shop.

She climbed the stairs to find her mentor behind the counter, fiddling with small pieces of metal. The Drow appraised her with mischievous glints in her eyes, and there was a note of amusement in her voice. "So you still don't care about the hair, huh?"

Diana sighed. "Yeah, yeah, whatever. I had a late night. Is there anything to eat around here?"

Nylotte shook her head. "Nope. We'll have to go out." She finished adjusting the items and extended them to her. "More charms. One is a replacement multiples illusion.

The other is something that should help with the tentacles if they appear again."

The agent took the shaped metal pieces and secured them in the leather bracer that protected her wrist from getting burned when their magic was consumed. They slid in beside the shield charm the Dark Elf had given her after the ambush attack. *It wouldn't have helped, though. I wasn't wearing the bracer.* She'd learned her lesson, and the thick cuff was now a constant accessory to all her outfits.

Her teacher preceded her out the front door of the shop, then turned to physically lock it. Diana felt a touch of magic as the Drow waved to activate the wards, which were significantly more dangerous to an intruder than they had been before the enemy attack on the building. They walked slowly down the street and took the long route to the main thoroughfare rather than cut through one of the connecting pathways. Stonesreach was full of life and activity and beings of every magical kind went about their lives in the city-under-the-city.

"Why does Lechnas want to rule the kemanas?"

Nylotte shrugged. "Why does anyone want to rule anything? He might lie to himself and ascribe noble intentions—perhaps the preservation of magic on this inhospitable planet—but in the end, it's about what it's always about. Power and the acquisition thereof."

Diana raised an eyebrow at her mentor's philosophical statement. "It seems like you've thought about the matter a fair amount."

That the other woman understood she was referring to power in general, not the current situation in particular, was evident in her response. "I've never been interested in ruling anyone other than myself. Well, and perhaps a student or two. But it's impossible to ignore the impulse in others." She gestured with her arms as she warmed to the topic. "It's so obvious, despite their efforts to conceal it or the inability to recognize it in themselves. Alayne is a good example. I have no doubt she believes every decision is made in the altruistic best interests of her people. But if stepping down and letting another rule was the best option? She'd make a different decision."

She nodded. It was consistent with those she'd met who were at the top of their ladders. "Maybe that gets less true as you move down the hierarchy. I can't see Bryant holding on to the job if he thought someone else would be better at it."

The Drow shrugged. "Maybe. Maybe not. Maybe it's a factor of how long they're in power for. Anyway"—she pointed at a building to their right—"let's pause the conversation for a while and have lunch."

"Breakfast."

"For normal people, it is lunchtime."

Diana laughed. "If I'm anything, normal is definitely not it."

Her companion grinned. "I couldn't have said it better myself."

The restaurant was much the same as those above ground. Of course, the lights were magical, the decorations tended toward the gothic, and the servers were nonhuman but otherwise, the trappings were the same. Tables were arranged in rows with reasonable space between them and various beings enjoyed the meals and the camaraderie. A few smaller tables were arrayed outside the front of the eatery, but as there was no wall facing the street, every seat was able to enjoy the sights and sounds of the thoroughfare. Nylotte led her to a table in the back row, and Diana perused the menu.

The reason for her teacher's choice was immediately obvious. In addition to all the unfamiliar Oriceran dishes, one page featured foods she recognized. They ordered and both selected a soup and main course. She opted for a bison burger, and her companion chose a salad with a fancy name. They talked about her training and took a tangent into magical theory she found both amazing and difficult to comprehend. Finally, when the kemana's version of coffee had been delivered, the conversation turned to more pressing matters.

"So, suggestions?" the agent asked. "Is there anything from the lady?"

The Drow snorted. "The palace is mostly useless, as usual. But they have confirmed an increased amount of chatter on the streets about the Remembrance attack and the names Iressa and Lechnas have been heard."

"They're surveilling the whole populace? Not only known troublemakers?"

Her companion shook her head. "Honestly, how you manage to be such a thorn in your enemies' sides while being so hopelessly naïve is beyond me. Yes, of course they listen to everyone. There might be a spy in this very restaurant at this very moment. Power, remember?"

She sighed. "Yeah. I guess I keep hoping there will be an exception."

"Continue to hope, but don't count on it."

"Right." She took a sip of the bitter brew and winced as it attacked her tongue. "Anyway. Do you have anything to contribute?"

Nylotte nodded. "We need to deal with Iressa and Lechnas decisively. Both at once if necessary, but separately would be far more effective. That is the crux of the matter. As long as they are free to pursue their quest for power, Stonesreach and your city are in danger. Not to mention the other kemanas and the cities connected to them."

Diana blew out a breath through pursed lips. "Well, that's no biggie. You and I can take care of that before dinner."

The Dark Elf chuckled. "Perhaps not. Even I would be wary of facing them singly, much less together. Plus, they'll likely be smart enough to keep their movements hidden by using pawns on Earth and maybe on both planets. Finding an opportunity will be a challenge."

"Can we create one?"

"Possibly. It's certainly worth thinking about. But although I hate to say it, we'll probably have to go outside normal channels to get a sense of what they're up to."

She regarded her with both caution and curiosity. "Like what?"

Her teacher sighed. "I know people—the kind who skirt around the edges of social acceptability. I can reach out but there will be a cost to it."

"So, I need to let some more magical evidence slide off

the books?" The initial arrangement to compensate Nylotte for teaching her had long since become an informal trade of favors, but she still routed some of the most interesting or most dangerous items to her. She had no idea what she did with them and had decided she definitely didn't want to know.

"At a minimum. But it'll probably cost more than that."

"Like what, exactly?" she asked with a frown

"Obligation."

The way she said it indicated a far deeper meaning than the ordinary interpretation of the word. "That sounds kind of ominous."

A single nod confirmed it. "The kinds of beings I'm talking about take debt very seriously. Failure to pay in the coin of their choosing would result in a nonstop flow of attacks. As long as enough people owe them, they can spend the obligations freely until the debtor is dead."

Diana shuddered. "Well, that's cheery." She took a bracing sip of her coffee and froze her face to stop it from twisting at the taste. The caffeine, though, was entirely welcome. "If it's what I have to do then it's what I have to do. I'll trust you to know when we reach that point."

Nylotte drained her cup in one hasty movement. "The problem is that it's unlikely it will only be you on the hook. The danger involved in seeking information about Iressa and Lechnas is significant, so the price will be as well. No offense intended, but the people we're discussing likely won't consider you talented enough to fulfill the full cost of the debt. They don't know you like I do."

The twist on her teacher's lips left it unclear whether she was being sincere or subtly insulting her. *Probably the second stacked on the first. Nothing's ever clear with her.* "I wouldn't ask you to do that."

The Drow waved a hand dismissively. "I don't require your permission on this matter any more than I do on any other. If it's necessary, I will. If it's not, I won't."

What hadn't exactly been said was the other woman's desire for her student to explore her heritage and to continue to learn from her, but it was all there under the surface. The Dark Elf had plans for her, clearly, that hadn't yet been shared. *But they can't come to fruition if I'm dead. Thank heaven she's not a necromancer.* "Has anyone ever told you that you're a hardass?"

A grin spread across her companion's features. "Once or twice. It seems that's another thing we have in common."

She locked her gaze on her mentor's and paused to ensure Nylotte was focused on her. "Whatever debts need to be incurred and whatever actions need to be taken, I won't stop until Lechnas and Iressa are out of the picture and you are out from under whatever it costs to get us there."

Her mentor nodded. "Then it's past time we got to work. Sooner begun, sooner finished."

CHAPTER FOURTEEN

The early evening patrol pattern for today was high on the list of Rath's favorites. Although his efforts had mostly moved to the evenings when he could soar unseen above the city's nighttime activities, the walks where Max served as his mount were special. They reminded him of the earliest days when he'd been learning about his new homes, first in the other city and then in this one. Of the two, he preferred where they were now, even though he missed Lisa.

He patted the Borzoi's head and grasped the collar more firmly as the dog ran happily forward. They wove in and out of people on the sidewalk and occasionally took to the grass to avoid collisions. Their path led them toward the place where he'd first seen the Silver Griffins, having followed Professor Charlotte there. The pedestrians and traffic decreased the closer they got to the house, and he decided there was no reason to not take a look at it. He believed it belonged to the most reclusive member of the group, who hadn't made an effort to introduce himself. *Or there could be more members than I've seen. I never thought to ask.*

The home was brightly lit and even welcoming. He considered knocking on the door but didn't want to disturb anyone inside. Instead, he guided Max to the window he'd looked through on his first trip there and expected to see several of them gathered around the table while they chatted and drank out of delicate china cups. His smile of anticipation vanished when his mount lifted him above the windowsill.

The table was there and the chairs on each side of it, but two were askew and two others knocked over. One of the teacups was in pieces on the floor, and the others had been upended and had spilled their contents on the table's surface. The best-case scenario was that they'd had to leave in a hurry. The worst case...well, he didn't even want to contemplate what that might be.

"Front door, Max."

The dog raced around the corner of the house, recognition of his rider's worry apparent in his rapid movement. The troll slipped off and grew to his three-foot size, strapped his utility belt and batons on, and twisted the handle. It was unlocked, which only increased his concern. *But if they left quickly, they could have not done that part. It's possible.* He pushed the door open and crept cautiously inside but raised a hand to prevent his partner from following. In the silence, he swept his gaze across the connected living and dining areas but no imminent threats were evident.

With a frown, he advanced to the table. Closer inspection didn't reveal any new information, and he blew out a frustrated breath. "Gwen, call Professor Charlotte."

Half a minute passed before his AI replied, "She doesn't answer."

Rath scowled. What had been a moderate sense of worry now rocketed to stratospheric levels. "Try Manny."

Another thirty seconds later, she said, "Emanuel is not picking up, either."

He made a hasty search of the house and his mind spun as he considered his next steps. It proved fruitless as well, and the troll returned to the living room, crouched on the back of the couch, and stared at the table. The Borzoi gave a soft bark through the open door. "You're right, Max. It does seem very strange." Their relationship had become close enough that he could interpret most of the dog's feelings as if they were words. Currently, his canine partner was perplexed. "No signs of a battle except for the spilled and dropped things, and the chairs."

He hopped down and circled the table slowly. "Probably not a physical force attack, then. More stuff would be damaged. And I don't see blood or anything." He tapped a finger against his chin, unconsciously imitating a detective from a movie he had watched with Bryant and Diana and Max. "Maybe drugs?" He climbed on one of the chairs. As part of the overall security increase, he'd been given a testing device that looked like a wand since the chip that the others used was incompatible with his ability to change size. He retrieved it from a holder on the back of his belt and touched the spilled tea with it.

Gwen's reply was almost instantaneous. "No danger."

He stuck the tester in the sugar bowl and the small pitcher of milk and received the same response.

"So. Not drugs. If they were attacked, that leaves magic." He turned to the dog. "Maybe they left? Got a call and gone quick?"

The Borzoi moved his head from side to side with a worried glint in his eyes.

"Yeah. Don't think so either. Gwen, track phones?"

A minute passed before the AI informed him there was no connection.

"Comms?"

A much quicker reply followed. "Emanuel's comm found but not receiving." The model they'd provided him with looked exactly like a hearing aid and in fact, served that purpose when it wasn't communicating. "Location?"

He frowned at the response, his fears confirmed. Emanuel's comm was located at the warehouse the Remembrance had used. *Someone's sending a message.* He considered calling for assistance but knew he could arrive before anyone else would if he hurried. "Let's go, Max. As fast as you can to the cathedral."

The troll launched from the spire and his flight suit wings snapped out to catch the air and carry him toward the Remembrance's former home. He focused hard to quiet the fear in his head and push all the terrible things that might be happening to his friends away. *The tea wasn't totally cold yet. I'm not that far behind them.* He descended slightly to capture a speedy breeze and wove in and out of building-top obstacles with as little movement as possible to maintain his velocity.

Theaters filled and restaurants blared music out their open fronts while he flashed over the city's nightlife. Ordinarily, he enjoyed the presence of those things. Today, though, he merely wished they'd speed by faster. He climbed higher as he neared his destination to avoid his approach being seen. Gwen plotted a descent spiral for him, and he followed it carefully, remaining inches outside potential sightlines from the holes in the roof that still hadn't been repaired. On the way down, heat signatures appeared in his goggles and revealed eight figures inside. Unintelligible words crept into the edge of his hearing as the AI worked to filter the important sounds from the random noise.

Rath touched down gently and pressed the button to retract the wings as he landed on the roof rather than a few feet above as was his usual acrobatic preference. Gwen superimposed a path that would take him invisibly across the top of the structure to the hole that provided the best angle on the scene below. He shrugged the flight suit off silently and tested the draw on his knives and batons before he crept forward.

The situation that greeted him was both better and worse than he'd feared. There were four enemies. One stood in front of each of his four friends, who were bound with heavy straps to metal chairs. He magnified his view and studied the Griffins. There were two he hadn't met, both men, seated in the middle of those he knew. The one with the long beard had blood at his temple. The sight caused the troll to clench his hands in anger and they tightened further when he saw that Professor Charlotte had also been injured. Her eyes were unfocused and her head lolled in a way similar to when ARES agents had gotten concussions.

He whispered as softly as possible, "Gwen, when the fight starts, call ambulances." Because there would be a fight. He wouldn't—couldn't—leave his friends in danger. The enemy on the left and across from Manny suddenly spoke. "You all thought it would be fun to mess with our plans. Well, now you'll get what you deserve." The wizard directed his wand at his bound prisoner and Emmanuel stiffened and cried out in pain. Even though the attack wasn't visible, it was clearly effective. The other captive he didn't know shouted, "Stop," and he, too, went rigid in agony as the mage before him responded with magical violence.

The troll checked his knives a final time. As he did so, his sleeve slipped out from where it had snuck under the illusion detection bracelet. The icy jolt caused him to freeze in mid-motion. As quietly as he could, he ordered, "Gwen, enhanced sensor sweep. Anything you can think of." The view in his goggles pulsed and shifted as the AI tested different options, and he saw a ghost flicker in and out. "Stop. Go back one." A small title in the lower part of his visual field told him it was an electrical activity detector that had caught the four additional figures hiding in the corners of the building. Presumably, they were cloaked in illusions blocking sight, hearing, and heat sensing. *Tricky.*

"I can't take eight on alone." A frown settled over his face as the full ramifications of the situation slipped into his brain. "It's clearly a trap." He sifted through his options and found none that he liked. "Okay, Gwen," he began but was interrupted by a harsh, electronically disguised voice in his comm.

"Incoming friendly." He turned to see Amadeo appear out of the darkness, clad in a night-black wingsuit like the ones people who jumped off mountains used. He pulled up and touched down in silence before he stripped the suit off quickly to reveal his normal garb beneath. The assassin crouched in position and spoke quietly over the channel that connected them. "I've watched this group for a few days. Their leader is on my list. I assumed some of your team would show up when they went after your elderly friends."

"Who are they?"

The man gave a slight shrug. "Low-end wizard scum available for rent cheap. I assume someone you don't like has tasked them with attacking whoever responds."

Rath grinned. "Can turn tables. Will call others. We can all work together."

A shake of the black-masked head accompanied the response. "No. I'll work with you but not the others. One of them might decide I'm a problem and I'd have to kill them. You and I have an understanding. I can live with that."

"Eight on two?"

"Take it or leave it. If it's only me, I'll shoot the one I'm after from here and be done with it. He's hiding in the far corner. That will probably cause the others to panic and kill your friends. But since I get more if I bring him in alive, our objectives are in alignment. You'll be my distraction, and I'll be your backup."

He grinned. There wasn't much of a choice, and truth be told, he didn't wish to put anyone else at risk. Missing explosives had been mentioned around headquarters. For all he knew, the building was wired and the whole thing was a trap. His friends were his responsibility, not theirs. "Outstanding. Ready when you are."

A nod. "Okay, here's what I want you to do."

CHAPTER FIFTEEN

The plan wasn't complicated. Amadeo would shoot the man across from Professor Charlotte—the farthest of the visible four from where Rath stood—as the troll dropped into the building on the rope the man in black had brought. He finished attaching the line to a pipe that protruded from the roof and uncoiled it as he walked over to the hole.

"Gwen, if I am seriously injured, contact Diana. Also, don't forget the ambulances." He was confident the battle would be over quickly enough that the assassin could get clear with his prize before they arrived.

The distorted voice was loud in his ears. "Go."

The soft puff of the silenced weapon's discharge was barely audible in his amplified comms, and the wizard on the far end dropped without knowing what had killed him. His allies spun to different vectors in search of the source while they raised their wands to summon shields. Amadeo fired several more shots to cover his partner's descent, an unexpected act of teamwork that allowed him to reach the floor unnoticed. The nearest enemy—the man who had hurt Manny—faced in the wrong direction. *Too bad, scumbag.* He drew and hurled two of his four knives and they struck one above the other in the back of the man's neck. He made a startled sound and fell forward onto his face.

Three enemies were near enough to pose a threat—two in front of him and the single adversary in the corner at his left. He surged toward the latter, the feeling of another unaccounted for hidden enemy behind him, even at a distance, distinctly uncomfortable. The wizard lifted a wand and fired a blast of lightning at him, but it grounded on the magic deflector in his vest. Unfortunately, it also destroyed one of his two crystals, which meant his foe was impressively powerful.

He didn't squander the opportunity the death of his defensive item bought him but vaulted upward while he drew his batons, spread his arms wide, and whipped the weapons at the man's temples. The wizard panicked at the sight of the troll attacking his face and raised his hands to block. The batons hammered into his adversary's forearms and bruised or cracked them, but that was merely the distraction. Rath snapped his foot out in a kick that broke the wizard's nose and drove him stumbling back. He landed and jumped again, this time angling his weapons ahead of him. They struck his target in the chest and he twitched in a heap, a victim of the stun pads on the tips.

The troll landed and spun, knowing the remainder of the enemy would be on the move. At least three were down with maybe five left. He couldn't account for Amadeo's efforts but assumed the assassin would track his quarry first and only divert for targets of opportunity. Once he had the leader, though, he might assist with the rest of the trash. Both the wizards who'd tormented the Griffons were on their way toward him and the one in the lead already raised his wand. Fire erupted from the tip in a wide cone he had no chance to evade.

He gritted his teeth and sprinted into it, hoping the deflector would protect him even though he knew he couldn't count on it. His size increased with each step and his belt and vest pulled apart at the Velcro fasteners and fell away as he attained four and a half feet. When he reached seven, he was in the face of the wizard, whose eyes were as large as basketballs at the sight of the mammoth and very angry creature that had stepped from the flames. Rath punched him in the forehead, a deceptively simple blow with the power of his twisting hip driving it. The man hurtled toward the one behind him, who jumped hastily to the side and deflected the living projectile with a swipe of his wand.

A flicker appeared to the right and the troll ducked and tumbled out of the way in time to avoid the force blast that would have removed his head from his shoulders. He bounced up with a growl—the movement slower and the sound far more menacing than at his usual size—and circled to put the closest wizard between him and the other. A gunshot followed by a scream from across the room indicated that Amadeo was busy with his part in the fight.

The nearest enemy attempted to target him when the one farther away grinned wickedly and shifted his aim to Emmanuel. Rath lunged in front of the lightning before it could reach his friend. The shocks made his muscles twitch and burned his fur but otherwise, generated more pain than damage.

Before he could counterattack, the other wizard caught him with a force blast that catapulted him ten feet to impact the wall at an angle. He bounced off to land on his face, stunned for a moment before he scrambled forward to avoid the follow-up he knew must come. The wash of flame warmed his feet as he vacated its detonation point and began to shrink. A patch of black with a glint of silver on the grey concrete floor caught his eye, and he turned at an angle that would bring him toward it without revealing his intent. More assaults followed and he wove and feinted to evade them easily as the return to his three-foot size made him far more agile. When he was finally close enough, he dove for the vest and snatched up a knife.

He rolled onto his feet and threw. The wizard in front smirked when he realized the blade would miss him, but he wasn't the actual target. The blade struck true and pierced the face of the other wizard below his eye. He immediately toppled and his screams suggested he was out of the fight. That left the troll with one in front of him and another unaccounted for. The one who currently smirked at him seemed unconcerned about the fate of his ally and ejected tentacles from his wand that covered the troll and buried him in darkness.

Diana had talked about her experiences with the shadow tendrils but he hadn't fully understood. This time, with all the external light shut out, the dark did indeed seem to try to smother him and to wriggle into the nooks and crannies of his mind and fill him with doubt. Fortunately, he wasn't the kind of troll to spend too much energy on self-criticism. He thought of Max, Diana, and Kayleigh, and as his grin widened, so did his form. The tentacles squeezed as he grew in size and struggled to restrain him, but he continued to grow. Finally, at a foot larger than he'd ever been before, they were weak enough that he burst out of them and yelled in triumph. He looked at the small figure before him who brought his wand to bear and roared, "Rath Smash!"

The shocked look that filled the man's face before Rath's fists pounded through the shield he hadn't quite managed to raise was deeply satisfying. He crumpled soundlessly, and he kicked his ribs to career the wizard across the room and into a stack of empty crates. Amadeo appeared, dragging a bound man on a line behind him. He held a nasty-looking gun in one hand and the cable in the other. With a brief nod, he acknowledged the remains of the wizard who had rocketed past him. "That's a nice trick."

He grinned. "Sometimes, it's good to be big."

The assassin nodded. "I could use that kind of talent now and again. Would you be interested in taking on a few side contracts?"

A laugh escaped him as he began to return to his preferred size. "We make a good team. But different priorities."

"If that changes, you can leave a chalk mark on the entrance of the graveyard. Black chalk between blocks. I'll contact you."

He fastened his goggles and AI collar into place, and Gwen announced, "One minute on EMTs." Rath rushed to his vest and drew his last knife before he darted to

Manny's side. He peered up to find the assassin staring at him and tilted his head toward the front door. "Ambulances on the way."

The black mask stretched again to reveal his grin. "I'm aware. I never enter a battleground without surveillance." He drew a device from behind his back that resembled Rath's grapnel shooter attached to a pistol, secured a line he pulled from his belt to it, and aimed it at one of the holes in the roof. "Stay safe, troll."

"You too."

He nodded and fired the line, which quickly lifted him up and out of the building. The troll cut his friends free and returned the knife to his vest. When the paramedics entered the room, he directed them first to Professor Charlotte, whose head still lolled like she wasn't fully present. He exchanged words with the two he didn't know, gathered his fallen gear, and followed Manny out the doors and into a waiting ambulance. As the uniformed men were getting his friend situated, Rath whispered, "Gwen, have someone pick up flight suit."

"Watcher dispatched." Several of the watchers— different than the ones that delivered his equipment when he wasn't near one of his preset launch points—now had the ability to retrieve what he couldn't. When the medic left, he asked Emmanuel, "What happened?"

The man shrugged. "We were having tea and chatting when four wizards broke in. They used some kind of magic to lock our muscles and floated us here through a portal. As much as they enjoyed inflicting pain for no apparent reason, I don't think it was us they were after."

Rath nodded, uncomfortable with the idea that his

friends had been hurt because of him and his team. "Trap. For us."

Manny raised a grey eyebrow. "That guy back there a new member?"

The troll laughed. The stress of the battle had begun to ease and sought a way out. "Not quite. Professional acquaintance. Maybe friend."

"Seems dangerous."

"Entirely. But only for bad guys. Or those who cause him trouble."

His friend wobbled slightly and lay back on the stretcher. "Mental note. Don't upset the man in black."

Rath hopped down and headed to the doors before the reappearing EMT could close him in. "Good plan, man." He was distracted from watching the vehicle depart by the growl of a powerful engine. Gwen announced, "Boss," as Diana kicked gravel up with the car she'd bought to replace the destroyed Mustang, a new model dusky red Dodge Charger Hellcat with black on the hood. The power window descended, and she looked at him with a grin. "You look like someone who needs a shower and a dash of fondue."

He considered staying to help the Griffons but turned to find the last ambulance speeding away. Now, it was merely the cops and the bodies. He grinned, twirled into a gleeful flip, and ran to the vehicle. Diana was right—cheese, meat, and chocolate were exactly what he needed.

CHAPTER SIXTEEN

I f there was one thing Nylotte hated with every fiber in her being, it was having to negotiate from a position of lack. Most of her life had been an effort to avoid that and to come to any discussion armed with the right incentives or threats to give her an advantage. It was a system that had never failed her, not once. *But sometimes, the need is too great, and when that happens, you're the one who's screwed.*

If there was a second thing she hated, it was having to go to the other's stronghold, which carried with it a third— being required to dress in a way the other expected rather than as she preferred. The Drow sighed as she stared at the usually locked portion of the enormous armoire that held her dressier outfits. These were ones she'd wear only for her own enjoyment or because she was thrice damned.

She had to seek information from one of Oriceran's most weaselly wizards. This individual kept a not insignificant number of Willen in thrall by various means and used them to search for knowledge he would put to use in diverse schemes. She had met Chadrousse on several occasions and found him equal parts charming and disgusting.

Heh. I could say that about most of the wizards I've known. She selected the leather pants folded on the bottom. There were created from the skin of a bear-like creature native to her home planet and imbued with designs that, if properly invoked, could help channel defensive magic. They had cost as much as anything she'd ever had in her shop and rarely saw the light of day or even the purple-tinted illumination of the kemana's false day. The Dark Elf tossed them onto the small sofa in her dressing room and turned to the collection of garments again.

Something red, I think. Obvious, but restrained. A sense of danger, but not an outright threat. Nylotte pushed hangars aside until the long coat she'd thought of first was revealed. It was simple but striking, with a stiff mandarin collar and large ornamental buttons down the front, and reached almost to her ankles. She tilted her head speculatively and finally decided it might be too formal. *But with the top open and a black tunic beneath it—perfect.* She dressed quickly, added two high, lace-up leather boots that stopped immediately below her knees, and left the jacket unbuttoned.

The response to her request for a meeting—he no doubt thought of it as an audience—hadn't specified that she keep her weapons at home, and she wasn't about to deviate from the letter of the law in anything concerning the information-broker-slash-manipulator. Each boot had a sheath along the back that took a long custom poniard with a disguised hilt and no crossguard. She slipped on a wide belt that looked ornamental from the front beneath her unbuttoned jacket but held slim, shallow implements that wouldn't be visible under the outer garment. An emergency wand, a healing potion, an energy potion, and a few small round smoke bombs slid easily into their waiting receptacles.

Under her right sleeve, a punch blade strapped to the bottom of her forearm in a quick-release sheath. On the top of the arm rested a long dagger, oriented hilt-down for a cross-draw. On her left forearm, she wore a leather bracer reinforced with chain whose thinness belied its strength. It would absorb a sword strike without parting. All of those were backup plans, of course, for the powerful Drow. Magic was like breathing, a fact of her existence bound up in every cell. If she was forced to resort to the physical weapons, it would be a clear sign that matters had progressed extremely poorly.

She buttoned the coat slowly and focused her mind for the battle to come. This would be a fight solely of words, ideally, but a battle nonetheless—and one she intended to not only survive but win.

The Dark Elf had been provided an anchor point for a portal and despite her misgivings, it would be inappropriate to refuse her host's hospitality. She conjured the rift and stared through, impressed with the home revealed beyond it. *It seems like Chadrousse is doing well and not afraid to let others know it.* In his position, she would have kept a much lower profile and enjoyed her comforts without visible sign of them. Then again, she'd never believed she had anything to prove to anyone. Perhaps the wizard didn't share that confidence.

A single step brought her through to the other planet and the opening dwindled quickly to nothing behind her. She expanded her senses and felt the other places she knew —locations she could portal to if needed. Before her, the house stood on a wide grassy area, the nearest neighbors a thousand feet or more away on either side. Magical lights dotted the outside and enhanced the attractive architectural features. It was based on the gothic style, with wood accents to warm the stone skeleton of the place. A path consisting of steppingstones embedded in white sand meandered through bushes and flowers on the way to the front door. She had a momentary picture of the man's servant Willens acting as groundskeepers and snorted. That put her in the right frame of mind for the discussion to come, and she strode forward resolutely.

The double doors—bright blue and vibrant in the noon light—parted before she reached them. No attendant was present, so she wandered into the large foyer and paused to gaze at the elegant tables and pedestals and the items positioned on them. A Kilomea skull had been gold-plated with an emerald in its left eye socket and a sapphire in its right. Two daggers looked as if they might be artifacts. *He's probably trying to pretend he has Angel and Demon. Everything about this man is a pretense.*

At intervals along the black-and-white marbled tile of the floor were spots of red. They glowed softly, one after the next, in a pattern she assumed was to indicate which way to go. She sauntered in that direction and studied the large paintings on the walls that depicted people and scenes from the history of the planet and the conflicts that had consumed it at various times. Like the other things she'd seen in the home, they offered a suggestion of culture and sophistication that was quickly undermined by the flaws in the pieces themselves. *It might be deliberate misdirection. It wouldn't be smart to underestimate him based on all these trappings.*

The walk from the entryway to his receiving room led her down a hallway that ran the length of the house. It fit what she expected from him in that it exposed his visitors to evidence of his affluence in an effort to force them to consider the skill it took to acquire it. Another person might be overwhelmed or at least impressed. For Nylotte, however, the display was tawdry, common, and entirely in keeping with what she knew about the wizard.

When she turned the final corner into the doorway that opened to an opulent den, she was unsurprised to find him in a reading chair pretending to be deeply engrossed in a visibly ancient tome. The sharp cheekbones and dark eyes were as she remembered, although the skeletally thin face she recalled had fleshed out somewhat. His body was still far too narrow to be healthy, though, even accounting for the slimming effect of the black suit he wore.

He shrugged his long curled chestnut hair out of the way, closed the manuscript gently, and set it aside as he rose with a grin. "Nylotte. It's so good to see you." His syrupy tone reminded her of why she generally associated him with a queasy stomach.

"Chadrousse. A pleasure indeed. Thank you for the invitation."

He gestured at two small couches in the center of the

room, an offer to select her seat. She chose the one that faced the wall, which forced him to occupy the more distracting seat that looked out the windows onto a beautiful garden. It was a petty gesture but also a declaration that she wasn't impressed by what he'd shown her so far. He sat with a nod that seemed to indicate understanding. "So, what can I do for you? It's been a long time since our paths have crossed."

She nodded. "Indeed. Years, I believe. It was the anniversary party." Many Oriceran natives had held private celebrations to mark Rhazdon's defeat, and their last encounter had been at a particularly lavish one. She'd used the opportunity to cultivate new professional contacts. Her final sighting of him had been as he led a server off toward the hosts' bedroom.

The wizard leaned back, crossed his legs, and interlaced his fingers over a knee. "Yes. A disappointing affair as I recall. But, to business. What does the ever so independent Nylotte require?"

Maybe reminding him of the party wasn't such a great idea. Now that I think of it, he might have made a play for me that I rejected rather ungently. She shrugged internally. *Whatever.* "I've run into a situation you might be able to help me with. Naturally, I could take care of it on my own, but I have so many things going on that time has become an issue. In this case, it might be better to pay with gold instead of missing opportunities while doing it myself."

A smile revealed that not a word of what she'd said had fooled him. "Of course. I am at your disposal. Do tell me how I can help you."

Sigh. "A simple matter. Information on a wizard and on

a witch. It's probably an hour's work for you, if that."

His teeth were perfect when he showed them in a grin. "Some hours are far more costly than others, as you are well aware. Even now, the clock ticks."

"I seek knowledge about Lechnas and Iressa. Locations, plans, weaknesses, and anything relevant."

"You have set yourself against them?"

She smiled. "You know better than to try to gain anything from me for free, Chadrousse. What will you pay to find out?"

The wizard laughed. "And that is why I have always appreciated you. The blades never stay hidden for long."

Tempt me a little more and you'll see real ones, twit. Her thoughts didn't affect the smile that curved her lips. "Indeed. We are alike in that."

Chadrousse nodded. "I don't need to know what you're up to. I can certainly find that out in other ways if I wish to do so. So, the cost of the knowledge you seek will be considerable."

"I expected as much."

"Fortunately for you, I also have a need at the moment. While you are perhaps not as unique a supplier for me as I am for you, for this particular task, you will do. I would offer the information in trade for a service plus a Rhazdon artifact—or objects of equal power and a small pouch of diamonds."

She shook her head. "Please, Chadrousse, I was not born yesterday. That should be an 'or,' not an 'and.' An act of service, or the other items."

"Ah, but I perceive that time is of the essence for you. It is not so for me. I could wait for another to come along. I fear that you cannot. So the price is as I said." He sighed and waved a hand. "Okay, we are old friends. I will make an exception for you. The task within the fortnight, a medium pouch of diamonds, and a small pouch of rubies. The ones from the planet you inexplicably choose to live on have such an intriguing brightness to them."

Her body and most of her brain seemed to agree that drawing one of her boot blades to stab him through the throat would be the best way to finish the conversation. Despite this, she forced her fake smile to grow a touch larger. "Acceptable, if you can get me the information I require in a day."

He laughed. "I already have it, Nylotte. Did you think I wouldn't know what you wanted before you told me? You shall leave here with everything you need if we have an accord. Do we?"

"We do." *One day, the tables will turn and I will crack you like an egg, you prick.*

"Excellent. A drink to seal the bargain." He clapped his hands and made a gesture in the air, and a tray with two elegant glasses and a bottle of deep-red wine appeared on the small end table in the corner of the couches. He poured and offered her the choice of one, and she accepted. The liquid was smooth and delicious, perhaps the first true sign of his affluence and potential good taste she'd seen since her arrival.

"So, what is it you need me to do?"

He set his glass down and showed a smile that seemed genuine. "I believe it may challenge even your impressive skills. It involves breaking an innocent person out of Trevilsom prison."

CHAPTER SEVENTEEN

Diana shook her head. "Seriously, the trouble is coming from every angle lately." Lisa nodded from the other side of the dining room table in Diana's family home in Washington, DC. *It's much more her home than mine, now. I should talk to my parents about selling it to her.* The blonde had circles under her eyes and appeared substantially the worse for wear from their late-night carousing at the Beagle the evening before. *She looks like I feel.*

Her BFF lifted her coffee mug in two hands, took a large sip, and coughed a little as she set it back on the table. "It's all your fault. I told you tequila was not a good idea."

She laughed. "I'm not talking about the bar, and when did you get to be such a lightweight, anyway? I was discussing the world."

Lisa shook her head. "I have to agree. My company has become totally secretive. I have the same clients I've always had but no new ones. Strangely, for a law firm that makes money by billable hours, that doesn't seem to bother anyone. Plus, the partners spend most of their time in locked-door meetings. Who knows what they're doing?" She snapped her fingers and pointed a finger at Diana's nose. "Hey. You're a spy. You can get me one of those James Bond listening devices so I can find out what's going on."

"That would be crazy. More danger is not what you need, and that's what you'd be asking for. They could be mobbed up or something—a big bucket of worms. Look for a new gig."

"But I want to know." Her theatrical whine made them both laugh, and the woman sighed. "I think I'm a good lawyer. But I bet I could be good at many things. Maybe it's time for a different career or a change of scenery. Are you hiring?"

Diana rolled her eyes. "Yeah, no. That won't work out unless you've developed magical powers since I saw you last."

"You have normal people on your team, don't you?"

She chuckled. "Hey, ouch. We all consider ourselves 'normal.' But yes, we do have individuals who lack magic, but they tend to have been trained as agents or police or military or something."

Her friend clapped her hands. "I know. Start a legal division. We'll grind your enemies to fine powder through the courts."

A slight feeling of desperation slid in and she lowered her throbbing head to the table while the other woman spun her vision for what an ARES prosecutorial office might look like and why it was a brilliant idea that she create one that very day.

Carson Taggart was technically still a hospital patient, but it was clear he wouldn't be for much longer. The man had regained his former energy and only the fact that his muscles were not fully recovered kept him moving at a pace she could match without running as the three of them walked together through the public corridors leading to the huge atrium in the center of the building.

The garden space had been donated by someone wealthy and important decades before. Despite ongoing financial challenges and the need to expand the hospital's footprint when it was already hemmed in by neighbors on all sides, it had thrived. Several trees reached toward the piece of sky that showed through the four walls that bounded the verdant area, and a multitude of bushes and flowers grew in carefully curated arrangements. It smelled green, and Diana inhaled the serenity and let it course through her body like a balm to areas roughened by the use of her magic.

The only rules of the location were respecting others' solitude by remaining reasonably quiet. The ex-ARES head strode to a bench in an out of the way corner and sat between him and Bryant. He spoke in a low tone that wouldn't carry beyond his guests' ears. "You've come to bust me out of here, right? I have numerous different plans. The one with the highest probability of success will require Bryant to impersonate a female nurse, so I hope y'all brought an extra gallon of makeup because that'll take serious work."

She laughed. Bryant sighed, a long-suffering sound that produced a smile on their former superior's face. She replied, "While I would like to see that, your departure may have to be delayed for a while. In fact, you might want to change rooms and get a new name while you're here."

Taggart shifted his gaze to her. "Is it that bad?"

"There are already bounties on two of us." She shrugged. "It's not difficult to imagine that once one of our enemies has a moment of clarity, they'll realize spreading that around to a few more targets would make life harder for ARES." Bryant had kept his ex-boss up to date on all the teams' activities, despite the other man's repeated assertion that he was retired and didn't need the details.

"Bah." His response lacked vitriol and was offered more for form than any other reason. "I'm not important enough to matter to them."

Bryant chuckled. "Your current living arrangement seems to argue against that, boss." He'd explained that he continued to use that title mainly to be irritating, and to judge by the older man's expression, it seemed to work. "Anyway, better safe than sorry, right?"

The older man kicked at a loose stone on the gravel pathway and spun it into a nearby flowerbed to startle a bird hiding there. It chirped sharply, clearly offended, as it relocated to another side of the captive garden. "Fly free, little friend. You don't have to be trapped here like the rest of us." He sighed and his tone turned businesslike. "So, what's the deal? You wanted to talk privately and this is the most secluded corner in the whole damn place."

She'd activated her signal jammer as soon as she was positive that they were clear of any equipment it might hinder and presumed Bryant had done the same. They were as safe as they could ever be unless there was someone with a directional mic in one of the windows that

AGENTS OF VENGEANCE

looked down on the location. *Or a damned drone.* Both agents had been irate when they'd learned how the opposition had managed to subvert their security. She raised a hand to cover her mouth to defeat optical surveillance and lip-reading.

"All signs suggest we're nearing a tipping point. Before, the enemy seemed content to take their time. Now, everything seems really urgent. The attack on me, the planned one on Cara, and even Rath's friends, for God's sake. It all smacks of the desire for fast, fatal results."

Bryant nodded and spoke behind his own raised hand. "It looks like we need to bring Project A up to ready-to-deploy status. When something breaks, it'll likely be a surprise since our intelligence on them is virtually nothing now that the human pawns we knew about are imprisoned, scattered, or dead."

Taggart nodded and looked at the ground. "And what are you looking for from me?"

"The last piece of the puzzle," Diana answered. "The one you've held back."

He shook his head. "Finley didn't tell you?"

The other man scowled. "He's a paper tiger now. The VP cut his legs out from under him. He doubtless has access to that information but probably doesn't want to give up the game by doing so while eyes are on him. I'm sure you all have protocols and whatever surrounding it. But I know you well, boss. There's no way you didn't manage to take a look."

The former head of ARES seemed to have an internal discussion based on how his face twitched and shifted between expressions. Finally, he released a large sigh. "Yes,

I have some information but it's imperfect. I don't have the final destination, only the rally point and the number to call when it goes down."

Diana nodded and lowered her hand as she mirrored his posture to stare at her boots. *Damn. They need a shine.* "Maybe it's time to give us that information in case you decide to vanish to whatever island you've bought with the government money you've embezzled."

He frowned. "Y'all aren't supposed to know about that. Damned kids, always sticking your noses where they don't belong." Half a minute passed in silence before he nodded. "Okay. You're right. If Finley is no longer completely reliable, we need to have a different plan handy. The rally point is a warehouse Bryant knows. He once complained to me that it had a lingering scent of FBI."

Bryant's eyes widened. "No way."

Taggart laughed. "Yep. You were correct about the government but wrong about the division."

"Bloody hell. That's a fair trek."

"Not as long as the one afterward, from the little I know. If you have to disappear, you'll need to call a number and ask for Johnston." He put his hand between both of Bryant's and after a moment, he nodded. The man, who seemed rather energized for someone who'd recently been in a coma, turned to her and extended his hand. When she covered it with hers, he tapped a number onto her palm, pausing between each digit.

She grinned. "Cool trick, boss. You really should come back to work. Bryant isn't even fit to clean your office, much less hold it down."

Taggart shook his head. "Nope, I'm headed for my

island. Oh, wait, I've said too much. I meant Florida. That's where all the retirees go, right? Orlando, maybe, so I can visit the house of the mouse whenever I feel like it."

They stood and escorted him to his room, watched for trouble along the way, and found none. The goodbyes were hasty but heartfelt. As they walked into the plaza outside the building arm in arm, Diana leaned her head on Bryant's shoulder. "Do you have everything we need?"

"Yep."

"And do you know who Johnston is?"

"Nope."

She sighed. "Let's hope we never have to find out. I have to say, though, it sure as hell doesn't seem likely things will work out that way."

He redirected her toward a black ARES SUV that had pulled up at the curb. "I agree. That's why we'll go back to the base where we're confident of the security so we can plan this thing right. Now that we have a destination, it's time to determine how we make it there without dying in the process."

CHAPTER EIGHTEEN

Lechnas had chosen the ruined courtyard for their meeting to remind the witch of her past failures as a way to focus her mind toward their common goal. When he materialized on its perimeter, he stared around curiously and wondered what the battle that had ravaged it had been like. He envisioned the opposing sides and gauged the positions he would have deployed his people in to make use of the space most effectively. He could almost see it all in its former grandeur.

With a shake of his head, he walked slowly toward the dry central fountain the circle had used for its gatherings. When he'd suggested the location to Dreven, it had been for its remoteness plus the hope that the man might learn something about the hubris he seemed blind to. In the end, he hadn't learned and had died at the hands of those he underestimated. *Perhaps I chose this place for my meeting for a similar reason—to remind myself not to misjudge Iressa.*

He arrived at the circle and took position as the witch's portal opened with a hissing sound. She stepped through and banished the rift, and he tracked her movements as she walked toward him. The sway of her hips, whether deliberate or merely automatic at this point, would definitely have been interesting if he were not so focused on his purpose. But he was, so it wasn't. "Thank you for coming."

She laughed. "Why in the world did you choose this desolate ruin? Are you depressed or something?"

He shook his head but couldn't prevent a smile from twitching the ends of his lips. "No, I simply thought it might make for convenient neutral ground. My home is inaccessible to others at the moment." He had fully invoked all his defenses when reports of his name being whispered in the shadows reached his ears.

A slow frown crept onto her face. "That sounds ominous."

"People I trust—reliable beings—have informed me that both you and I are of interest to someone or someones."

"On Earth?"

"No. Here."

Iressa pursed her lips and was silent for a moment, clearly deep in thought. "The humans wouldn't have the right access. So it's one of the Oricerans who are connected to them."

He nodded. "Either the Drow in their capital city or the one in Stonesreach would be my guess. Both are accomplished traders and would have the appropriate contacts."

The witch growled. "Perhaps we should remove whoever is working with those traitors on this planet as an example to anyone else who might consider doing so."

Lechnas shrugged. "In the grand scheme, it matters little. What's important is that we don't lose focus on our goal. The best way to deal with any threat is not to hide from it but to eliminate those bold enough to believe they can accomplish it."

"Do you mean more bounties on more people?"

He made a neutral gesture with his hand—half-lift and half-point. "As a way to add a little pressure, certainly. But we can no longer trust others to accomplish our plans. It is time we commit fully and take care of it ourselves."

Always one to prefer misdirection and manipulation to overt action, she looked unhappy at his words. She stared at the ground for a full minute and he didn't break her silence. *At some point, we all must face the repercussions of our choices. Now is her time.* He moved his hands behind his back casually and let the wand in his right sleeve slide into his hand.

Finally, she seemed to come to a decision and raised her gaze to his. "Good. Chipping away at them has been both unsuccessful and annoying. Let's be done with it."

He tapped the wand into its sheath once again and allowed his arms to fall to his sides. "Excellent. We are in agreement, then. The only question is how we approach destroying our enemies. My first thought is that we start with the kemana but focus specifically upon the palace. If we can remove Lady Alayne, our path forward becomes far easier. Perhaps the next person in the line of succession will be more amenable to our priorities."

"And if not, we simply kill them all until we find one who is. It seems like a good plan to me. What resources do we have?" A soft breeze played with the ends of her hair and distracted him for a moment with ideas of what might be possible between them after their plans for conquest were concluded. He crushed the thought. *This is not the time.*

He shrugged. "Kilomea muscle can be bought, contracted for, or coerced. Warriors are not a concern. Wizards and witches are harder to recruit, but there are at least two dozen who would respond immediately to my summons and the same number who would comply with minimal convincing. You may have access to half the first group of magicals for an initial assault on Stonesreach and as many Kilomea as you feel you need."

She frowned, probably at the notion that the responsibility for attacking the kemana was hers. "Will you join that effort?"

"No. I shall plan for the one that follows—the one that will eliminate the humans who aren't killed by your assault. Of the two, it should be the more difficult task as they have proven both resilient and unpredictable. Plus, you have had more than enough time to eradicate them through your pawns but have been unsuccessful. It may simply require a different perspective."

Her frown deepened. "You're oversimplifying that particular situation, but whatever. When do you want the first event to occur?"

"Within days. Say three days from now, at sundown in the city above the kemana. I'll arrange for the witches, wizards, and Kilomea to portal to a place of your choosing, and you can direct them from there. When you have taken Stonesreach, our foes above will be weakened. We will permit them enough time to grow afraid and eliminate them."

Iressa nodded and when she spoke, her voice was

noticeably colder than it had been. "Very well, Lechnas. See that you live up to your commitment."

"Of course, Iressa."

She stalked away, summoned a portal, and vanished. He shook his head and spoke to the empty courtyard with a disappointed sigh. "One must work with the partners one has, regardless of what one might wish for." *I'm sure she's thinking the same thing right about now.*

Iressa materialized in the home she'd purchased on Earth through a series of middle-persons. This was located in a remote section of the country's mid-west. Since portals covered great distances in an instant, she felt no obligation to be close to the action in Pittsburgh except when absolutely required. *Unfortunately, that bastard Lechnas has declared it is now required. And then some.*

When she'd first accepted the invitation to join the circle and later, when she'd agreed to work directly with Lechnas, leading an army personally into battle was definitely not among the things she envisioned doing. Nothing had changed since then, but she was more or less stuck with the task now. If she sent a proxy and they succeeded, it would diminish her in the wizard's eyes and he would almost certainly and justifiably break their partnership. If a representative failed, he would be entirely within the bounds of propriety to kill her for her refusal to accept her responsibility.

She walked from the small entry room through her living and dining rooms on the way to the bedroom. There were only six pieces of furniture in the whole home—dining table, couch, coffee table, bed, dressing sofa in her walk-in closet, and nightstand. The emptiness of the space appealed to her and the white walls and open atmosphere soothed her ever-present sense of being trapped. That feeling had been with her for as long as she could remember but had grown exponentially since her involvement with Lechnas and his minions.

Even if I could go back, I'd probably do the same thing again. She sighed, turned the handles on the double-sized bathtub, and poured a capful of lavender oil into the stream of water. A trip to the closet to deposit her clothes in the basket to be washed and retrieve a robe was the only remaining task, and once it was completed, she sank gratefully into the steaming hot liquid and let her eyelids drift closed. The heat was a balm to her muscles, especially after the always chilly courtyard. She snorted inwardly. *Why he chose to meet there instead of someplace decent is beyond me.* She considered that further. *But he doesn't usually do anything without a good reason. So what was the purpose?*

Her mind examined possibilities but failed to find any worth latching onto. From there, her thoughts turned to practicalities and strategies to win a battle in the kemana. Eventually, she forced herself to consider the possibility of defeat and what would come after. *What can be gained if we fail to kill Lady Alayne?* She answered herself out loud. "Well, there is considerable treasure to be had in the palace. That's something."

Her mental voice countered, *We can steal treasure whenever we like. How is that useful?*

She frowned. "I can't believe I'm arguing with myself.

Maybe I really am losing my mind. Not money treasure. Magical treasure. Artifacts. Power." She sensed agreement from the other side of her mind. "Right. That's something. If we used the attack in part as cover for snatching whatever magical items or weapons they have hidden in the castle, we'd have a victory even if the little wench gets away. And if we manage to kill her, it's a double win."

What would Lechnas think of that plan?

"Screw him." She laughed. "There's no reason he would know and if I do decide to share, it'll be a triumph." There was no response, and she laughed again when she realized she was respectfully waiting for her imaginary counterpart to say something.

Iressa slipped under the surface, held her breath, and let her arms float freely. Lying embraced by the warmth made everything seem okay and confirmed that her plans were the best she would be able to come up with. She lost track of time, emerged to breathe only when absolutely had to, and added hot water to maintain the cocoon of comfort as often as necessary until it ran out.

Later, dressed in sleepwear and with her hair dried and bound in a ponytail to keep it out of her way, the witch climbed into bed. Her mind had moved from its restful state into its normal practical planning mode, and she mentally cataloged the things she would need to make the attack successful. *What I really must have is a little more clarity—inside information about the palace. And, as near as I can tell, there's someone who owes me for shooting his mouth off.*

It had come to her in a flash. The obvious identity of the individual who worked with one of the two Drow associated with their enemies was Chadrousse—exactly the kind of person who would take such a contract and believe himself untouchable by virtue of his ability to serve and/or blackmail anyone who had an issue with him. She smiled as she pushed her face into the pillow. *Heck, if he tells me what I need to know without causing me to work for it, I might even be willing to let him live. If he has something good to offer me in trade. Possibly.*

She fell asleep and her dreams were filled with visions of the attack on the kemana. Each ended with her sitting primly on the throne wearing Lady Alayne's jewels. The woman herself lay at her feet and the only variation in the dreams was whether the pathetic leader of Stonesreach was cowed, broken, or dead.

CHAPTER NINETEEN

The black SUV drew up beside the rented warehouse on a side street in the city's strip district. Inside, hidden behind the physical walls and electronics galore, was the BAM mobile armory. Diana had passed the word down that it was time to ensure the vehicle was ready for a road trip with the additional requirement that it must be a fully capable base of operations rather than simply a supplement to their headquarters.

Hank slid out of the passenger side and Cara exited from the driver's seat. The boss had detailed her second in command to work with him on the final checklist, an assignment neither of them had a problem with. The respect they'd already had for one another when she'd brought him into BAM Pittsburgh had only increased with the passage of time, particularly given their shared interest in the fight club. He didn't think Anik was an entirely suitable partner for her, but he also didn't think it was his place to offer a comment, especially since he wasn't interested in the gig.

He typed in a sixteen-digit access code and the garage door rolled up. Lights turned on automatically two stories overhead to illuminate the wide space holding only the eighteen-wheeler that was their rolling command post. "So, do you know what the deal is with the new requirements? Other than the boss says so, that is." Her word was enough for them, but he wouldn't mind a little more context if it was available.

Cara shook her head. "Not really. Putting various snippets together, I'd say there's a concern we'll need to take our show on the road. It could be in support of another ARES group, maybe DC. Then again, it might be something else. Possibly, she simply wants to keep her options open. Who the hell knows? Ours is not to reason why and all that."

Her teammate nodded as he walked to the back and palmed the sensor. The step folded down automatically, a new feature he'd added a week before, and the doors swung wide. The interior lights powered on, connected to a separate battery that charged when the vehicle was running or by power from a heavy-duty cable attached to the grid like it was now. He scrambled inside and called, "Ralph, status."

The truck's speakers emitted a rough voice that seemed to suggest the stereotype of a trucker over citizen's band radio, despite the clash in terminology. "Nominal."

She lifted an eyebrow. "Ralph?"

He grinned. "Yeah, because when we're using the armory, we're gonna Wreck It. Not the armory. The enemy." She chuckled and he growled. "Shut up, you."

With another hearty laugh, she scrambled inside behind

him. They made their way from the back of the truck to the front. She called out components from the checklist on the tablet she carried and he pointed out where the items were stored so they could make the mandated visual inspections. They started with the pistols and rifles on the wall near the doors and worked forward to check each locker and the weapons storage above the seating bench before they finally reached the medical area.

"Marvin, full check of supplies," Hank called.

After a brief pause, the dour voice replied, "Full supplies confirmed. Epinephrine stores will expire in eighty-nine days."

Cara looked questioningly at her teammate and he nodded. "We resupply at sixty." She nodded and tapped keys. He said, "Marvin, full diagnostic." The delay was longer this time—almost a full minute—before he replied, "Nominal. All systems functioning within expected parameters."

She held the tablet behind her back. "I believe you've omitted an important part of the inspection."

He adopted an innocent look. "He runs fine so there's nothing to worry about there. The thing is brand new."

"You know what I mean." She shook her head. "Time to uncover what's up top."

"I'm not sure you're cleared for that level of knowledge." He grinned. "Would you care to show me your orders?"

Her growl wasn't entirely playful. "If you don't do it right now, we'll have our own little fight club here in the warehouse and you will not enjoy it."

"On the contrary, I think I would totally dig that."

Cara couldn't hold the glare and laughed, and he hopped out of the truck by way of the medical section door. He retrieved his own tablet from the cab and pushed through the security checks, then held it out to show her the display. "Okay, this controls all the toys on top, although we can do it via voice or through any of the AIs, too. Deacon's computers in the passenger seat will handle it, as well."

Diana's order to include the tech's equipment had been fulfilled by locating it in the cab, the only place where there was still unallocated space. It was cramped but serviceable. Primary connectivity came from a satellite dish that tracked a government bird in low orbit. The secondary source was a combination of onboard access to local cell towers and hijacking whatever bandwidth was nearby. Deacon had designed the code for the latter and was quite proud of it.

But not as proud as Hank was of the toys he was about to show his teammate. "So, here's the first." One button slid the panel aside and the second lifted the drone out of its hiding place and commanded it to hover above the truck. "It's the fastest model we have with stun capability and two rockets—miniature versions of the sidewinder. Fire and forget once it's locked on."

He cut his gaze to the side to watch her eyes widen in surprise. "Holy hell. That's something."

"Yeah, we required a deterrent capable of hitting a home run if we're being pursued. This is it. We have two reloads for the rockets on board but changing them while we're moving would be action-movie caliber. If we hadn't needed the medical bay, I could have done it, but that rightfully took precedence."

"Who runs it when we're in motion?"

"It's Diana's call, or yours if she's not here." He shrugged. "If it's up to me, whichever passenger is the best shot."

She looked at it in admiration and shook her head slightly like she wasn't able to believe it. *Heh. If that has you stoked, wait.* She refocused with a visible effort of will. "Okay, what else is up there?"

When he pressed another button, the panel at the back of the vehicle opened. The defensive cluster rose into view, an array of weapons mounted on a spinning half-sphere.

Cara whistled. "I'm very sure I see a stun weapon there. I presume it's powerful enough to fry drones?"

Hank nodded. "Unless they're hardened but hopefully, the military won't be the ones chasing us."

"What are the other two normal barrels and what is that big one?"

"One of the smaller ones is smoke, and the other is actually oil."

"You're kidding me."

He laughed. "Nope. It's like Spy Hunter from the eighties but even better because the big one is a canister launcher. We have a three-way feeder, with caltrops, incendiary, and fragmentation loads."

She grinned. "Did they give you a blank check and you crammed in every teenage boy's spy fantasy you could?"

His expression a little sheepish, he scratched the back of his neck. "Well, yeah, basically."

"Color me officially impressed." She laughed and it had a slight edge of disbelief to it. "Geez, man. Nice work."

"And now, the crown jewel." He pressed the required buttons and a turret emerged from the center. It looked much like the defensive cluster but was clearly designed for destruction. Two mini-guns were positioned at a ninety-degree angle from one another, and the top held four missile rails with two birds aimed in each direction. He put it through its diagnostic sequence, which resulted in impressive spinning by the turret as a whole and by the mini-gun barrels in particular. "The seekers are active homing, with a designator lock-on controlled by Ralph or any of the other interface systems. If needed, they can bounce to satellite to maintain the designator."

"Holy shit. Seriously. I knew you were good but this is amazing. How did you do it?"

Hank shrugged and pressed the buttons to secure everything again. "I know people. Good people. We do things for each other. I guess I called in more than a few favors I was owed for this. Plus, having ARES' resources made most things easy. What really did it, though, was the fact that you all trusted me to handle it. If I'd had to check in on every last thing, it would have never come together. There was simply too much that I had to change on the fly."

Cara was openly impressed by the enormity of the machine's power. "Well, however you did it, you should be really proud of yourself."

He laughed. "Oh, I am. Don't doubt that. False humility is not a thing for me, and Ralph rocks hard."

"Most guys would have named this the Terminator Ten Million or something like that. You choose a kids' movie."

"I'm not most guys."

She chuckled. "You can say that again."

He tossed the tablet into the cab and climbed up after it. The engine turned immediately, and he activated the heads-up displays and control panels that would let him manage the vehicle. In truth, it could run autonomously if needed. But, while he loved technology, even the AIs didn't have the uniquely human intuition that so often made the difference between success and failure.

A broad grin on his face, he pulled the mobile armory out of the warehouse. The programmable skin on the sides, back, and top proclaimed it to be a delivery truck filled with a particularly boring brand of beer. This ensured that no one would take particular notice as it rolled through the city streets towards its destination, a covered parking lot near enough to the ARES headquarters to have it in action two minutes after they discovered a need. He couldn't shake the premonition that they'd have that need sooner rather than later.

CHAPTER TWENTY

If there was one thing Nylotte had not expected to wake up to, it was a message from Chadrousse that used words like "immediately" and "urgent." Even more unexpected was the fact that he asked to meet in a neutral location rather than summon her to another session at the home that was a testimony to his success. The appointment was in only a half-hour's time, so she needed to move from her bedroom to a location she'd never visited on Oriceran and do so in a hurry.

The situation was weird enough that she snatched up the same pants as before—the leather ones that could be employed for magical defense at need. She strapped on another belt, this one with obvious pouches holding useful items, thankful that she always topped it off no matter how tired she was after whatever she'd used it for last. For a moment, she worried that something had happened to hasten the timetable on the Trevilsom matter, but surely he would have mentioned it if that were the case since that particular adventure would require far more equipment. No, this was something else.

The Dark Elf pulled on a tight black tunic Diana had given her and a looser, dressier one over it. She donned the high lace-up boots with the poniards in the back and chose a leather jacket that had a few extras sewn into the lining. *Okay, I'm as ready as I can be.* She activated the wards and portaled out of the building into a small town in the Oriceran countryside. A tavern loomed before her, quaint and classic with an actual wooden sign hung on the outside. It featured a drawing of two dragons clinking flagons of ale together and was called the Drunken Dragons Inn. The paint was faded but the lizard on the left appeared to have once been bright green and the other gold.

Cautiously, she pushed through the heavy planked door and into a common area filled with a boisterous crowd. The bartender, an angry-looking Dwarf with shockingly white hair and beard, pointed at her and at a small doorway at the back of the room. She nodded and mimed drinking, and he made a shooing motion with her hands. Nylotte moved through the tightly packed revelers, her demeanor enough to keep the most drunken idiots but one from trying to grab her as she passed. That person—a wizard by the look of him—screamed when she caught his groping hand and channeled heat through his arm. Without even a glance at him, she yanked him from the bench and dropped him carelessly before she continued.

She pushed through the doorway, which was shielded by rows of beads strung from the top of it, and found Chadrousse at a table inside, half his face cradled in a hand.

The man looked strange, and as she grew closer, she decided "damaged" was a better word for it. The confidence he had possessed had vanished and he now appeared hunted—or haunted, possibly. *Maybe both.* Sarcastic words evaporated as she sat beside him. "What happened, Rousse?"

He laughed, and she heard self-deprecation in it. Clearly, something notable had occurred. "Apparently, word that I was gathering information on Lechnas and Iressa traveled a little further than I intended. The witch came for a visit while I was sleeping."

The Drow winced. Whatever would come after that kind of introduction wasn't likely to be good.

His voice trembled as he spoke. "She demanded information and I gave it to her willingly, free of charge. But that didn't stop her, no—even though she promised. It didn't stop her."

The proud man she'd met barely days before was gone as if he'd never existed. "What can I do?"

His laugh was darker this time. "I don't know. Do you have a spare eye?" He moved his hand aside to display a patch over his right socket, one that dipped deeply enough to reveal that there was nothing behind it.

"That's awful. I'm sorry. Truly."

He shook his head and grasped the handle of the cup before him but didn't raise it to his lips. "It's what I deserved. I was sloppy. I knew she was crazy but forgot how crazy."

Nylotte nodded. "Yeah. Really damn crazy, that one." She wanted to ask him why she was there but he seemed unlikely to be receptive to the question yet. He was too deep in his own head. "Will you be able to continue doing what you do?"

He lifted the drink, took a strong sip, and winced. As he lowered it, she saw that it was filled not with beer, but with whiskey. A great deal of whiskey. "Yes. As long as word doesn't spread that she did this to me, which is why I needed to speak to you." He looked up and his single eye blazed with anger. "I can't release you from the task we've agreed upon. I've already committed us both. But I don't need the diamonds or the rubies and I will owe you a favor if you do this one thing for me." She waited as he ground his teeth together before he forced the words out. "Get rid of her, and as painfully as possible. Do this for me." The next word visibly cost him almost everything he had left to give. "Please."

She was back where she liked to be, in control of the situation, but his circumstances had changed so dramatically that she couldn't bring herself to exploit the advantage. *Besides, he's right. That witch needs to be dealt with permanently.* "Chadrousse, you have my word. I will destroy her."

A thin smile crept onto his features and he seemed to relax as if a burden of some kind had lifted from him. "Good. Very good. You'll need to move fast, though. I've kept my ears open for any news, and various threads have come together. Whatever she's doing, the attack will happen soon—tomorrow at the latest. And everything points to Stonesreach as the target."

Diana was in her backyard, throwing a frisbee with Rath and enjoying the sight of Max trying to take a bite out of it each time it flew past his position. The hair on her arms raised in a way she associated with the presence of magic. Her right hand slid to her hip and her left came up in defense, and she turned toward a portal opening in the back corner of the fenced-in area at the right moment to be smacked in the temple by the flying disc.

"Ow, dammit," she groused as she kept her Glock and her power a hair's breadth away from detonation. Nylotte stepped through, wearing a killer outfit of black boots, pants, and jacket—all in leather—and the agent gaped in surprise. "Have you been out clubbing or something?"

Her teacher sighed and waved the portal closed behind her. "Get inside. We have matters of import to discuss."

While the Drow detailed everything she knew about Iressa and the upcoming attack, Diana listened carefully and expected to have questions or concerns at the end. But when the Dark Elf finished speaking, she felt no uncertainty and needed no more information. "You're telling me we know she's coming, we know where, and we have a reasonable idea of when?"

She nodded.

"Well, hell, it's like my birthday. Let me call Cara and Hank and we can start planning to give her a really rude reception."

CHAPTER TWENTY-ONE

After the initial warning, the afternoon crawled like a sleepy snail toward evening. Diana and Nylotte had concluded that there was a high probability that the attack would occur at night, both because it made tactical sense and because that's what Iressa had chosen for her previous assault on the kemana. While there was no way to predict what the crazy witch would do with any certainty, they were both confident about the timing of the event.

Hank, Cara, and Rath met her at headquarters to prepare for the battle in the technology-free zone that was Stonesreach. The vests with their magical deflectors were viable, and they checked them to ensure that the crystals were undamaged. The strap-on armor pieces were also good. Rath's batons might not shock his foes in the underground city, but they still packed a serious wallop when he put his speed behind them. The daggers in his vest were potentially deadly no matter where he was. A quick collaboration resulted in a couple more sheaths strapped to his belt in place of grenades, which increased his arsenal to ten knives. He grinned and quipped in a terrible Australian accent, "Now that's a knife."

Cara looked confused, Hank laughed, and Diana simply shook her head at the Crocodile Dundee impersonation. The troll's endless movie consumption had taken some weird turns lately. *Anything but Shatner. Please, no Shatner.* She practiced Fury's draw a few times and tugged on the bottom of the sheath to get the weapon angled properly. It was more a time-killing fidget than an actual need, and even though she was aware of that, she continued to do it until it felt perfect. She added a second healing and energy potion to her own belt, plus her guns at her hip and back. There was no telling how the battle would go, and it was always possible they'd be in a situation where the weapons would work. Extra mags went into their usual slots, all filled with anti-magic rounds.

Her second in command made similar choices, but with Angel and Demon at her thighs. Hank did the same, minus the daggers, but he added wicked-looking metal items to his gloves she hadn't seen before. They were modeled after brass knuckles but had two protrusions in the middle. She tilted her chin in a question, and he grinned. "I worked with Kayleigh on them. Where tech works, they provide a more concentrated shock than the gloves—about a third more power. But more importantly, no matter where I use them, they'll hurt the scumbags in ways that matter."

Diana cast about for other items that might assist in making Iressa's day worse but didn't locate anything. She shrugged inwardly. *We've got this. The equipment is important and useful, but in the end, it'll come down to will and no one will beat us there. Ever.* She summoned a portal to the training space in the basement of Nylotte's shop and wondered how the Drow's efforts at the palace were going.

Nylotte fumed quietly as she waited in the throne room with a dozen others who had been granted an audience with Lady Alayne. The numbers weren't the problem. The fact that the annoying prat in charge of the kemana hadn't bothered to show up during the hour since she'd entered was. When the woman's advisor had tottered off in search of her, she'd been sure the elf had understood the gravity of the information she had to share. The long wait suggested she might have misread his level of intelligence or awareness.

A couple of the others had attempted to begin conversations with her, but her dark scowl intensified when she turned it on them and they quickly found other discussion partners. She stood rigidly in front of the throne to claim the primary position should the woman ever choose to appear. A whisper in her mind gave notice that her basement warning wards had been triggered by someone recognized, and the confirmation that Diana and presumably her team had arrived made the waiting a little easier to bear.

Only a little easier—the tiniest fraction—but it was something positive. Her prevailing inclination was still to lay waste to everything and everyone in the room as a sign of her frustration. Finally, when she was almost at the point of being ready to let the kemana fend for itself, Lady Alayne appeared. The fear on her face wouldn't be apparent to someone less familiar with that particular expression, but it communicated itself clearly to the Dark Elf, who'd inspired it on many occasions.

Her advisor stepped forward and spoke formally. "This audience is now in session. The lady of Stonesreach requests all petitioners other than the Dark Elf Nylotte to please exit the chamber and await her pleasure in the antechamber."

She smothered the petty grin that threatened under the realization that this occurrence was not a good sign. Despite the impulse, she maintained her posture and her silence while she searched the eyes of the bejeweled woman before her and noted that the fear was in their depths as well. *Alayne isn't the best ruler, not by a long shot, but neither is she a coward. I wonder what she knows.* Finally, the doors banged closed behind her and a quick glance revealed that the guards who normally stood within the room were now also outside.

Alayne's voice held a tremble. "What news, Nylotte?"

She couldn't help herself, not after the long delay. "What news yourself, Lady Alayne? I have been here for an hour waiting—an hour that could have been spent preparing. Clearly, something of import must have delayed you."

A scolding for speaking to the nominal leader of the kemana in that fashion would have been appropriate, and when the other two exchanged glances, the Drow thought for a moment that she would receive exactly that. Then, Alayne made a sound that was half-cough and half-sob. "They tried to poison me. My half-sister is dead and I would be if she hadn't stolen a mouthful from my plate as a joke." Tears formed and fell but to her credit, she maintained her dignity, ignored them, and held her visitor's gaze.

Nylotte's anger softened. "I am sorry, my lady, for my words and tone, and doubly sorry for your loss. May her journey be swift and her arrival be a cause for celebration among your ancestors." She wasn't sure which version of the Light Elf afterlife the woman believed in so kept it neutral and applicable to all and received a nod in response. "Have you identified the culprit?"

Her advisor spoke, his voice soft but filled with anger, not remorse. "Two of the kitchen workers. They did not try to hide their actions and only expressed regret that they'd been unsuccessful. They're currently being questioned. Now, clearly, you are here for a different reason— an important one since you've waited this long. What is it?"

She frowned. "It's doubtless connected. Carefully cultivated sources tell me Iressa will attack Stonesreach sometime in the next couple of days."

"What are these sources?"

The Dark Elf shook her head. "You'll have to take my word that they are reliable unless you wish to open your own horde of secrets to me."

Lady Alayne cut his reply off. "We have every reason to trust you, Nylotte. Do you have further details?"

"Unfortunately, I do not. My allies have arrived in the kemana, and we will watch for trouble. It was my thought that perhaps we should anchor our defense here in the palace. They and I could wait in the front throne room, and you could coordinate our efforts with those of your own people."

The ruler twisted in her chair to stare at her advisor, and the older man twitched his head to the left and right. The stare turned into a harsher look, and he simply raised an eyebrow. The lady resumed her formal posture. "No, we shall secure this building against all but our most trusted from this time forward until we have come to terms with this attack. You, we would trust. Your human allies, although they have proven themselves useful, have no reason to prize our persons. They will not be permitted inside the palace while we deal with this betrayal."

"I don't agree with this decision, but I do understand it." Nylotte sighed. "However, I fear that in making what seems like the prudent choice, you are in fact making the least effective one. I would ask you to reconsider." Again, they exchanged glances and again, the advisor was unmoved. The woman in the chair before her shook her head. "Very well. I wish you good fortune and suggest you make certain all your guards are ready. The last attack on Stonesreach was led by someone with multiple objectives and a reasonable, if twisted, grasp on reality. Iressa is the opposite—entirely unpredictable and capable of intense single-mindedness. Of the two, I'd choose to face Dreven every time."

She turned and exited the chamber, growling internally at the effectiveness of the battle's subtle first move.

When the Drow banged into the shop looking irritated, Diana grinned from her position behind the counter, her pose exactly like the one she'd seen her mentor use so often. "Rough day at the office?" At her back, the ARES contingent chuckled at her clever barb. *Or my stupidity. One or the other.*

"You could say that. Someone tried to poison the lady and killed her sister."

She bolted up from her seat. "What the hell?"

"It has to be Iressa sowing chaos before her assault. Or Lechnas with the same purpose, but my coins are on the witch. Poison seems like her style."

"Damn. Pulling off an attack inside the palace. That takes serious patience."

Nylotte leaned on the counter to her right. "And planning. That's something Dreven never did well. He was all about short-term tactics—and good at it—but believed he was a better strategist than he was. She's the real deal for both."

"It would have been a mess if she'd succeeded."

"She did succeed, only not as completely as she intended. Someone like Iressa has multiple objectives for everything she does—a total win and a series of partials. While killing Alayne would have had the most impact, she's managed to put the palace in a defensive posture."

"But that's a bad thing for her, and a good thing for us," Hank interjected.

The Dark Elf raised her gaze from where she had stared at the counter to nod at him. "It seems like it would be, right? But it's already blocked our plan of coordinating the defense from there. Now, the castle is separate from the rest of the kemana. We're split into two disparate units that essentially can't communicate before the battle has even begun. Tell me, is that something you'd do in the field?"

He shook his head, his expression grim. "No. I see what you're saying."

The expressions Nylotte customarily wore were absent, and the usual mirth, sarcasm, and castigation were replaced by a look of worry that seemed sincere. Dianna noticed immediately and asked, "You seem worried—far more so than usual. Why?"

She sighed and shifted her gaze to her. "With Dreven, we knew the boundaries. But Iressa—aside from her almost insane single-mindedness—is as random as anyone I've ever come across. It's impossible to guess what's important to her at any given moment, which makes it equally impossible to know what she's going to do. For instance, will she come here to attack the palace? To kill every innocent civilian she can find? To raze buildings to the ground as a visible reminder of her power? It could be any or all."

Rath spoke in a dour voice that sounded entirely unlike him. "Some people aren't looking for anything logical like money. They can't be bought, bullied, reasoned, or negotiated with. Some people simply want to watch the world burn."

The elf nodded. "And like the Joker in that movie, she is a true wildcard. It's not chaos she wants. She always has a purpose, but I can't see what it is. Worse, I fear we won't know until the trouble she's planned has already happened."

Diana shook her head. "Then it's all the more important to strike so fast and so hard that she doesn't have a chance to do whatever messed up thing she has in mind. So let's quit whining about it and decide how to do it."

CHAPTER TWENTY-TWO

After much discussion, they had decided to establish a central position along the thoroughfare on one of the buildings with a roof sufficiently high to monitor the surrounding streets. Each of the ARES team positioned themselves at a corner and their gazes moved constantly across their ninety-degree portion of the circle in the hopes of detecting trouble the instant it appeared. Nylotte had remained at her shop, her telepathic connection with Diana strong enough down there that her teacher would know when something happened almost as quickly as she did.

"It really is pretty down here," Hank said. "They could make a killing on tourism."

Cara laughed. "We could put a creepy amusement park run by Drow in that corner."

Diana shook her head but couldn't contain a laugh when Rath added, "Featuring troll jousts. Max would love it." It was good that her people were loose and she wished she could be the same. She wasn't tense as such, merely impatient. In those moments where her mind was free to do what it wanted, it gave her a suffocating sense of the enormity of the situation and the realization that she and her team were in a hurricane, not a rain shower. The other members of BAM Pittsburgh were assembled at the base, ready to deploy by mobile armory or helicopter if something happened on the surface. Kayleigh and Deacon had promised to put all the tech and skills they possessed into watching over the city they all loved during this critical moment.

She wondered idly what the information had cost Nylotte—both the initial details and the revelation of the attack—and recommitted to helping her mentor pay the bill, no matter what it was.

Her second in command jolted her out of her head with a shout. "Look at the palace." She darted to the opposite side of the building as portals appeared directly outside the grounds of the castle, which confirmed beyond doubt that this was the primary target. Invaders poured out and the unexpected sight of the hulking Kilomea prowling among them revealed that the enemy had come ready to battle with both magic and muscle. She squinted and thought she saw wands when magical attacks erupted to batter the transparent shield that protected the kemana's leader.

"Dammit. Exactly like Nylotte suspected." She'd believed the Dark Elf but they'd both agreed that the best call was to watch the entire city in case she was wrong and that it should be done without using any arcane skills to avoid giving the enemy premature warning that their attack wasn't a complete surprise. "Let's go, people."

The others threw the ropes anchored in the center of the roof down on the side that led to the main street, and Diana leapt groundward, using her force magic to control her speed until she touched down gently on the cobblestone.

The Drow let her know she'd join them when they arrived, and when her teammates descended beside her, they sprinted together toward the gleaming white building at the end of the cavern. They received strange looks from the people in the restaurants and shops but continued in silence. There was no point in alerting anyone who wouldn't be able to help for fear they'd get involved with the best of intentions and only make things worse.

Nylotte had gathered a group of the stronger talents who lived in Stonesreach and put them on notice, charging them with the task of defending any area where Diana's team wasn't. Ideally, they would now spread out into the streets of the kemana to guard against any additional attacks or overflow from the action at the palace. As the battle on the front steps came into sight, Diana cleared all the other thoughts from her head.

What she found was more or less what she'd imagined. The outer shield around the grounds had fallen and the enemy had separated into two forces. The first fought for control of the space before the large doors that had been damaged in the previous battle. They were faced by a phalanx of defenders in dark metal armor whose shields were, so far, protecting them against the streams of magic thrown at the entrance and at them. The other group flowed unopposed through the narrow channel that she and Nylotte had used on their last visit. Scorch marks on the small openings visible from her angle explained why the palace guards hadn't bottled them up there as planned.

Dammit. Both are vital, which means we have to separate. She shouted, "Hank, Cara, go right. Hopefully, they'll be far enough ahead that you can sneak in a few attacks before they know you're there. Retreat if you feel threatened. Our main job is to survive the day, you hear me? Everything else is secondary."

"Gotcha, boss."

"Sounds good."

The duo angled toward that side of the wide stone platform. Rath said, "So many bad people."

Diana couldn't help but agree. "Yeah. Definitely. So our first attacks need to be decisive. No playing." She looked aside, saw his grin, and shook her head. *I'm not sure trolls are capable of sustained seriousness.* A hasty count of the enemies ahead led to the sobering realization that there were four humanoid figures with wands against ten defenders, and seven Kilomea ready for the slightest suggestion of a faltering defense. The interlocked shields of the palace guards, identical to the approach used in Roman times, was effective so far but realistically, it would only take one Kilomea to break it.

As if it had heard her thoughts, one of the large creatures backpedaled to gain distance before he sprinted forward and vaulted into a trajectory that would carry him into the massed guards. Spears snapped up to offer him a welcome, but a thin beam of flame washed across directly above the tops of the shields and sliced the metal heads from the wooden poles. When hundreds of pounds of flesh and bone landed on the center of the formation, the entire group shuddered but held. When the second Kilomea impacted only seconds later, the middle collapsed and it turned into a melee.

The defenders who hadn't been crushed under a mountain of massive creature spread out, seeking individual battles where they would be at an advantage. The numbers were momentarily against them but Diana and Rath immediately entered the fray. Her intention had been to wait until they were close enough for Fury, but when the phalanx shattered, she reacted on instinct. Both arms thrust forward and force blasts erupted from them, one each at the head of the wizard on the right and the Kilomea on the left, who had one of the black-armored guards on the ground under a foot. The former was leveled by the blow, and the latter was knocked aside far enough for his victim to roll free.

Rath hurled knives, his accuracy perfect even at top speed. The first two pierced a witch's neck and arm and felled her instantly. The second brace caught a Kilomea who held a raised ax. His abrupt turn was the only thing that preserved his eyes from the blades that quivered into his cheek. The two remaining wizards spun and attacked, far faster than those who had been with the Remembrance before had proven capable of. *Damn. We have the A-Team here today.*

She used a force blast to elevate both her and Rath, a move they'd practiced in the backyard. He twisted in mid-air, drew his batons and brought his feet under him, then landed behind a distracted Kilomea. Lightning-fast strikes to the sides of the knees and the bottoms of the elbows demanded the hulk's attention.

Diana lost sight of that battle as she pushed herself telekinetically to avoid a cone of shadow that passed beside her head. Two casters were so busy trying to land effective assaults that they didn't fully realize her destination until she landed directly in front of them. The one on the left squealed and encased himself in ice before she could strike him. His partner tried to bring his wand around in an attack.

The agent snapped a sidekick into his groin that thrust him away and disabled him in the next moment with an uppercut that shattered his jaw. The absence of the snap that heralded a stun glove activating was notable and weird. She spun to the ice cocoon and used a thin line of fire to drill through it at sternum height. With nowhere to go to avoid it, the mage dispelled the ice and raised a shield to block her flame. His defensive instinct opened himself to a simultaneous double blow to the knees from Rath, who stood behind him.

The wizard crumpled and the troll put him out with a blow to his temple. The numbers were now much better, but the defenders needed help with the bigger creatures so the ARES duo waded in to assist.

Cara stepped back as Hank moved in front of her to take the lead down the narrow passage. They'd worked together often enough that most things were automatic—like the fact that he couldn't punch from behind her, but she could definitely shoot fire darts past him if needed. They made it down the deathtrap alley without meeting opposition but discovered a very different situation when they pelted around the corner.

Ahead, where Diana had described the entrance, a semicircle of guards with tall shields stood with them interlocked. Kilomea battered at them with blades, clubs, and fists but were no more successful in piercing the defense than the wizards and witches who sent fire, lightning, and shadow into them. Anything that arced overhead was eliminated by bolts of magic from unseen defenders inside the protection of the half-ring.

When Cara and Hank stopped to assess the situation, illusions fell and Kilomea lashed out at both of them from either side. She barely managed to get an arm up in time to block a punch aimed at her face and her partner went down under his attacker. A cone of shadow reached for her as she bounced off the wall and she dropped, rolled forward under it, and darted up with a back kick aimed at the pursuing giant's knee. He twisted and took it on the leg, which felt vaguely like kicking a stone barricade. The brute pounded a fist onto her thigh. The limb snapped and she collapsed in a haze of pain.

Hank bellowed and hurled the giant off him in the direction of the wizard who had shot at her. He bounded to his feet and stalked toward her opponent, blocked a punch and a kick like they were too slow to worry him, and delivered a short, vicious jab to the creature's face that caved it in. Cara saw the setup and the effects, but the actual blow was so fast she couldn't track it while she fumbled for one of her healing potions. She downed it, screamed as her bone knitted itself together, and managed to roll out of the way of the next shadow blast that only narrowly missed her.

Her partner's eyes blazed when he looked down to check on her before he turned to rush another group of invaders. The defensive position had lost cohesion and the battle had devolved into individual fights. A flash caught her attention and she saw a figure dart inside the doorway and ran to follow. Two Kilomea stepped into her path and each pointed a two-handed greatsword at her. She slid to a stop to avoid impaling herself and discovered Angel and Demon in her hands with no memory of drawing them. The enemies swung their blades down at an angle to create a V with her feet at the point they planned to meet.

The daggers whispered a strategy and she circled them up and out and deflected the huge weapons to either side. She surged forward while they were out of the way and delivered a front kick to the knee of the one on the left, crushed the joint, and dropped him.

The other disengaged from her block and whipped his sword in a horizontal strike at her ribs. She was caught flat-footed and barely managed to summon a fire shield in the wrong-side hand and twist around to intercept it. The power of the blow was such that she tripped and flailed into a witch, surprising them both. She drew her head back and snapped it forward with all the strength she could muster to shatter the woman's nose. The sword came in again, and she dropped low to evade. The blood spray drenched her as it sliced through the witch's neck.

Dude. Gross. She bounced up again and stabbed with both daggers, one high and one low. He blocked the one aimed at his solar plexus with the hilt of the sword but only managed to twist away from the other. Instead of a groin strike, the blade punched deeply into his thigh. She ripped it out sideways and was splashed with more blood as the artery found a new outlet.

"Cara," Hank bellowed from a few feet away and she turned in his direction. *Smart move, not scaring me with a touch.* The sight beyond him was shocking. Every one of the defenders was down, most of them bleeding with limbs twisted in directions they weren't supposed to go. He was limping. "What the hell happened?"

"Some kind of magical explosion death spell. It struck in waves. If I hadn't been under a Kilomea at the time, I'm sure I'd be dead." He shrugged and she noticed that his metal knuckles were stained.

"I saw one of the invaders run inside."

"Not only one. I saw a few too."

She cut a reasonably clean part of her uniform shirt and used the inner portion to mop icky stuff that didn't bear thinking about off her face. "I guess we need to follow whoever it was." She retrieved an energy potion and drained half, then handed it to Hank, who finished the rest. The effect was immediate and all but convinced her she was ready to confront all the enemies in the palace single-handed. They dashed into the castle and made short work of the two Kilomean guards who had remained behind to stop them.

"Where do you think they're going?" her partner asked

A loud crash sounded from ahead and to the left, and

they sprinted forward to investigate. Diana and Rath stood on two giant doors that had apparently toppled inward and crushed what appeared to be at least one more Kilomea. The boss sounded ticked. "They're after Alayne and Nylotte says most of the defenders have already been killed. It's up to us to save her."

CHAPTER TWENTY-THREE

Nylotte had managed to veil herself and slip into the building with the invaders after she waited until a particularly slow on the uptake Kilomea left a gap in the inward flow. She'd watched Cara and her partner fighting and had been confident once the daggers emerged that everything would work out okay in that fracas. Not for the first time, she considered how nice it would be to have her own magical weapon. Also not for the first time, she concluded the endless chatter that came with owning one would make her chew her own fingers off to make it stop before more than a day had passed.

She'd followed the insurgents and heard Iressa give the orders to separate and search for Alayne and to steal whatever items of power weren't nailed down. It confirmed both her understanding of the other woman and her fears about the purpose of the attack. A telepathic message to Diana had ensured that she would defend the lady of the kemana, leaving the Drow free to find the right opportunity to squash the witch in the black dress like the insect she was.

Her invisibility had given her time to come up with a great plan to eliminate her foe at the moment of her apparent triumph and she was content to simply follow the raiders, ever giddier with anticipation, when the unthinkable occurred. One of the Kilomea she was shadowing tripped and she dodged to the side instinctively to avoid him. In doing so, she stepped between a wizard's raised wand and a ceramic bust of an unfamiliar Light Elf in the same moment that he shouted, "Take that." A cone of ice rocketed toward the sculpture on a trajectory that would take it directly through her.

With a heartfelt sigh, the Drow banished her illusion and summoned her own frozen shield. It intercepted the attack and bounced it back at the caster, who began to realize his peril when his own magic catapulted him into his comrades. The witches and wizards fell in a tangle and she couldn't help but laugh at the sight. "An invasion and a show. The best kind of night out."

Iressa snarled. "All of you, with me." She pointed at a cluster of casters and Kilomea near her. "The rest of you, kill that meddling wench." The narrow rectangular room was strangely calm as her foes rearranged themselves. Three Kilomea formed a front rank to protect a trio of wizards and a witch behind them. *Seven on one? You should have brought more of your cohorts.*

The Dark Elf bared her teeth and raised her arms. "Which of you is brave enough to be the first to die?"

Diana ran as fast as caution would allow in the direction Cara had seen the enemies heading, intent on tracking the witch down before she could bring harm to Alayne. Nylotte connected with her momentarily to show her the array of adversaries blocking the path several rooms ahead. She sent a hasty response, "Need help?" Their proximity in the kemana allowed for almost-real telepathic conversation, and she wished they could have it everywhere. It'd be far more convenient than hiring Willen as go-betweens.

The Dark Elf's condescending, "Please," was all the more powerful when the emotions behind it were transmitted mind-to-mind. "But take another path. This area won't be safe."

The agent diverted to the right and toward the main throne room and the doors inside that led deeper into the palace. When the four of them were halfway across the chamber, a wizard stepped through one of the other entrances. With a grin, he summoned a torrent of tiny icicles no larger than needles that pelted with hurricane force everywhere except where he stood. The BAM agents reacted instantly. Hank dove under the ornamental chair that served as Lady Alayne's literal seat of power, Cara created a whirling cylinder of flame around herself, and their boss summoned a dome of ice over herself and Rath.

The wizard's grin widened at the sight of their stalled progress. His attack continued until the moment that she lifted the shield enough for her diminutive partner to whip a throwing dagger at him. The troll's skill had developed to a level sufficient to account for the downward flow of the ice rain, and the blade pierced the man's throat with ease. He collapsed and the hail ended. They darted to the door he'd come from and Rath scooped the knife up without breaking stride.

They emerged into a wide corridor. On the far end to the left, Diana saw a flash of black that she instantly knew was Iressa. To the right, sounds of running feet suggested the enemy had separated again. There was no time to try to second-guess the situation. "Cara, Hank, go after that group. We're on the leader." Her sidekick laughed at the reference, and she shot him a grin as they pelted after the witch.

One of the Kilomea answered her taunt with a charge, and Nylotte smirked at the predictability of it all. She thrust both arms out and force blasts rocketed through the space that separated her from her oncoming foe. The shocked look that swept onto his face as he careened upward and backward was quickly banished by his impact against the heavy stone of the interior wall. He fell heavily and very definitely out of the battle. There was a pause that she interpreted as an impressed silence in appreciation of her magic before the others lurched into motion.

Well, that dealt with the most aggressive one, anyway. The ensuing battle was a dance as the elf wove and swooped among her enemies, free to strike with impunity while they had to worry about friendly fire. She twisted to avoid a cone of flame and laughed inwardly as it burned a nearby Kilomea, who responded with an offended growl. *Okay, literal friendly fire. What idiots.* She used her magic in short, surgical bursts to sometimes wield wickedly keen force blades to slice at tendons or blood vessels and other times, delivered a perfectly aimed crushing blow of force, shadow, or ice to annihilate an adversary.

One of the enemy wizards summoned a wave of shadow tentacles and accurately predicted her direction of movement so the appendages were able to grasp at her legs. She ducked under a slash from a Kilomea's sword and leaned aside from another's punch, and the wizard's words came clearly to her.

"They're too strong. You have no way to escape now, Drow." She pushed the tendrils up and down with her force magic enough to create a gap to push her arm through, then delivered a spread of five fire darts to his face. She had a deep respect for the way Cara had improved and refined the attack and had learned alongside her as she worked on it. Two of them burned through the wizard's eyes and both he and the tentacles fell away.

She had to abandon subtlety when the numbers thinned enough that her enemies no longer tripped over each other. Only a single Kilomea remained a few feet away from her with a scorch mark on the side of his heavy armor. Beyond him, a witch and wizard stood with wands raised, poised for an opportunity to attack. She shuffled to keep the brute in their line of sight and waited for him to make a move.

The shield in his left hand looked magicked, probably powered by one of the two behind him. If she threw something directly, it would give him an opening to attack with the double-headed ax in his right, which already had a crimson stain on it. He stormed toward her, but her anticipation of his aggressive approach allowed her to still her instinctive flinch and offer him a smile that communicated how pathetic she considered him.

Nylotte was aware that part of her foes' responsibility was to delay her to allow the others to accomplish their nefarious deeds unhindered. Apparently, this one was the opposite of the one who'd started the party, smarter than he was impulsive. *Okay. I can't wait any longer.* She dipped into her belt for a few tiny objects and hurled them to the floor in front of the beast, where they exploded into a cloud of smoke that quickly washed over his head. She summoned ice and spread it in an expanding circle from a point to the right of his feet. He slipped and fell awkwardly as a magical breeze pushed her distraction away.

The wizard looked surprised to be revealed. The witch's moving wand indicated that she was the one who had conjured the wind, and Nylotte rewarded her with an arm wave that flurried icicles from her hand in a curved arc at them. They summoned shields to block, and she turned her attention to the fallen brute while they were occupied. She made a motion akin to slamming her fist on a table, and his head bounced off the stone floor from the force bolt's impact. On the second attempt, he was ready for it and managed to keep the contact minimal. She compensated by using the same gesture but with hardly any power behind it, then used his resistance against him as the other hand brought a bolt from the ground to pound into his face and flip him backward.

The witch fired a cone of shadow at her and she created a buckler of the same magic to absorb it. The wizard chose force and launched a translucent beam at her knees, and she knelt and summoned a curved shield to redirect the attack at the witch's face. The woman fell like she'd been punched by a giant and the sound when her skull met stone resonated in the smallish space. He looked horrified at what he'd done in the instant before she forced him to choose between blocking the fire darts coming for his eyes or the force sphere that rocketed toward his groin. He tried to do both and managed to preserve his life but crumpled in agony from the brutal impact of the force magic.

The Kilomea was still trying to rise, his balance compromised by what was undoubtedly a serious concussion, and she crossed to him and applied her boot to his temple in a sharp kick. She assumed there was a fifty-fifty chance that he'd survive the encounter. The Drow repeated the process with the wizard and judged his chances lower. A quick glance into Diana's mind showed her running through a familiar part of the palace. After she'd retrieved the fallen wands, she raced toward the route that would bring her most quickly to her student's side.

Cara and Hank pounded after their quarry and narrowed the distance enough that a Kilomea turned to slow them. Hank delivered a straight punch that simply powered through the blocking arm and the skull behind it and his pace slowed from his effort to deal with the rear guard. It allowed her to take the lead, and when they turned a corner to discover a wizard waiting for her, she had sufficient time to summon a fire shield to put in the way of his shadow attack. She raced forward and stabbed Demon low while she raised the buckler to hammer it into him. The blade sank deep into his stomach. She thumped into him and knocked him aside, and Hank darted past her again.

He was a step in front when they broke into the broad open space the lady of the Kemana had chosen for her defensive position. She was in the corner farthest from their entrance near a door she could escape though, with her advisor beside her. They added their power to that of two elves in white armor who stood before them and maintained a shimmering shield that curved from wall to wall and floor to ceiling. A ring of guards positioned outside the barrier held large glowing physical shields and interposed them to thwart the Kilomeas' attempts to break through. In the rear rank of attackers, three wizards and a witch launched magical attacks over the melee to weaken the barricade protecting Alayne.

The enemy had some foresight, anyway, and a wash of flame greeted them as she stepped fully into the room. A second witch stood in the corner to her right and had obviously waited for their appearance. Cara absorbed it with a blaze of her own and fired her darts at the woman. Her assailant ducked to avoid them and delivered a force bolt at Hank, who had strayed beyond her protection. It struck and he fell, while one of the wizards noticed the exchange and turned to bring his wand to bear. She threw Demon at him with a sideways twist, then hurled Angel at the witch. Both summoned shields to block but it bought her partner the time he needed to regain his feet. He waded in on the wizard with fists and elbows as she charged the witch.

She was able to hurdle the first fire attack, slide under the next, and somersault over the third. *If only Rath was here to see that move.* She caught the returning daggers in her fists and stabbed them downward. The strength of her strike combined with the momentum of her movement to penetrate the woman's fire shield. The blades thrust deep into her chest and she went pale and fell. The agent spun and whipped both knives at the closest wizard, who was focused on his attack on the guards and didn't realize he was in danger until they thudded home in his back.

Suddenly, the shield faltered and a wave of Kilomea surged over the front fighters and fell on the white-armored defenders. One threw his ax, and she saw it catch Lady Alayne as she retreated through the door. Hank finished that one with a chop to the throat and together, they eliminated the others. The outer ring of defenders had been killed and one of the two personal guards was critically injured. She helped him to drink the healing potion he carried before she joined Hank in the adjoining room.

Alayne had blood on her dress but the chamber held a good supply of magic and the empty vials next to her assured Cara that she'd be okay. The woman reached out and touched her arm. "Thank you for coming to our aid. Please stay?"

There were many valid reasons not to, but she agreed anyway. "Of course, Lady Alayne. Hank will watch the room outside, and I'll remain here with you." He nodded, picked up the ax, and twirled it once in his hand as he stepped into the chamber. The relief on the Light Elf's face was confirmation that she'd made the right choice. *Hit that witch an extra time for me, boss.*

Diana and Rath finally caught up to Iressa in what could only be the palace's treasure vault. Chests of jewels and coins covered two of the four walls of the medium-sized space and tall shelves filled with seemingly random objects were set along the other two. The fact that the witch was in the center directing the quartet of wizards and witches as to which items to steal, rather than stuffing wealth into their bags, told her the objects were magical and powerful. She broke left and Rath moved the other way, and they immediately eliminated a wizard each with fire darts and thrown knives, respectively. The two who remained dropped their sacks and drew their wands, forcing the ARES agents to evade.

The troll went high and somersaulted over a line of lightning to clutch a shelf and hang from it one-handed. With the other, he threw a series of blades at the witch who had attacked him, but she knocked each aside as it neared her. He dropped, drew his batons, and barreled forward.

With a muttered imprecation, the agent rolled out of the way of the shadow bolts directed at her. She bolted to her feet and ran in an arc toward the witch in the black dress, ignoring her attacker. Iressa saw her approach and spat a curse, then generated a sphere of force around her that forced Diana to skid to a sudden stop lest she collide with it.

Rath whipped his baton across the nearest witch's wand hand. She lowered the slender rod and a force blade extended from the tip. It knocked his weapon away and slashed his face to trace a thin line along his forehead. The blood drops that fell in his eyes ratcheted his anger up, and he hurled his off-hand weapon at her. While she was distracted blocking it, two knives followed as quickly as he could draw and throw. She managed to deflect the first hastily but the second penetrated her arm. Her wand fell and she cried out, and the troll lunged forward and thrust up to hammer the baton against her head. When she crumpled, he turned his attention to the woman in the bubble.

Diana shouted, "Enough," when the frustration of it all surged over her. She drew Fury and raced toward the second witch, who'd attempted to strike her with shadow, and accepted an attack wave on her way in. Her teeth clenched involuntarily at the pain and violation of the magic, but it didn't stop her or even slow her. She sliced down with the sword at a diagonal and inflicted a deep wound from the witch's shoulder to her opposite thigh. Her foe's mouth opened and closed like she couldn't process what had happened, and she collapsed without a word.

Inside her protection, Iressa smiled—a smug expression that simply begged to be swiped off her face. The agent recognized the motions of her arms as a spell to summon a portal and pounded her sword furiously against the translucent barrier. She was desperate to stop the witch's escape, especially since the several objects at her feet looked very much like Rhazdon artifacts.

The circle completed, and the rift began to fill from the edges. Her gaze met her adversary's, which displayed both insanity and evil intentions in their depths. She realized Rath now also battered the shield at his largest size and his heavy fists hammered again and again on the barrier. She couldn't believe they'd come this far, only to watch her escape. It was too much to take, and she looked within her for something—anything—to stop the witch. There was nothing she could think of.

The next moment proved that her knowledge was incomplete. The portal spell reversed itself and fell apart before it could complete. A view of the room from an unoccupied corner appeared in Diana's mind, and she realized that not only was her mentor present, but she also blocked the other woman's ability to sneak away. The agent grinned.

"Stay on the sidelines, buddy, this one's mine. Unless you have a chance to hit her with a knife. That'd be fine." She didn't want anything to hinder her from going all out.

She knocked on the barrier with a smile. "You and me, bitch. How about you come out and we end this?"

CHAPTER TWENTY-FOUR

Rath complied with her instruction and edged to the doorway. He shrank and gathered his knife vest on the way. Her mentor remained hidden in the corner, veiled in illusion sophisticated enough that it didn't even trigger her detection bracelet. The field was clear for Diana to fight Iressa on her own if only the damned woman would emerge from behind her force barrier. The problem was, she seemed content to wait like she knew something they didn't. *Or maybe I'm being paranoid. Whatever. She needs to get out of there so I can kick her ass.*

Time froze around her and she thought it was her magic warning system responding to a threat. Before she could follow up on that, the avatar of her sword stepped into her field of view. He nodded at her. "Diana."

"Fury. This is new."

The figure in the elegant martial arts uniform inclined his head. "Circumstances demanded it."

She chuckled. "If you're capable of stopping time, you

could have shared that information sooner. It could have been useful, you know."

He smiled and looked wise and serene. "We are between one breath and the next, that is all. Slowed, but not stopped. Or, more accurately, you are sped up."

"Again, useful, secret-keeper."

"It only works for conversations, wielder." He laughed and she gestured for him to continue. "You can channel your magic through the sword. Do so, and it should cut through the barrier. And beware, for she is powerful."

Time resumed its normal pace, and the knowledge of how to accomplish Fury's recommendation was suddenly clear in her mind. Somehow, she knew that the best way to fight force was not by using any single magic but a combination of them. Digging deep, she summoned flame and lightning, twisted them together while she visualized them as an intertwined DNA strand, and squeezed them tighter and tighter. She pushed the power into the blade. It began to glow and flames and sparks hovered along the edge. She slashed it through the shield in a triangle, and the center portion fell away and vanished.

Diana grinned at the now very concerned-looking witch in the black dress who'd suddenly discovered that her house of bricks was actually a house of straw. "Do I really need to cut you out of there?"

Iressa offered no reply and instead, reached down for one of the magic items at her feet. She looked at Diana with equal parts crazy and fear in her gaze before she pressed the object down on the forearm that didn't already have a wicked-looking tattoo on it.

The pain as the artifact burned into her arm when she forced it to bond, rather than engaging in the persuasive dance that was the proper process, forced her to her knees. Outside, the woman had resumed the slow destruction of her sanctuary, but there was nothing Iressa could do about that—nothing she could do about anything until she mastered the artifact or it killed her.

There was a reason the existence of Rhazdon's Vengeance and Defense was so notable. Artifacts possessed part of the human who had empowered them, and they tended to be very jealous partners. Her existing artifact was no different, and the new one she'd attempted to merge with was, if anything, even more unwilling to share.

They immediately went to war and used her body as their battleground.

Time lost all meaning in the agony of the contest but eventually, she realized the words she'd screamed at them must have accomplished something. The pain receded to a level that didn't present an immediate threat to her sanity. She sensed reluctant acceptance that promised further battles to come as the two negotiated power relationships with her and with one another.

But right now, none of that mattered.

Right now, she had a human to kill.

Watching Iressa thrash and scream while she carved her way through the woman's defensive barrier was not something Diana ever wanted to experience again. She'd faced considerable pain, both physical and emotional in her life. Far more than average, anyway. But she decided that if she added it all up, it would be a stream compared to the roaring river the witch had been plunged into.

As she raised Fury for the decisive blow to the shield, the woman suddenly rose. Her eyes were fierce, and her face bled from where her own nails had raked it as she went through whatever it was that she'd gone through. Iressa tried the portal again—a last-ditch effort to avoid the conflict ahead—but Nylotte continued to block her. Her shoulders rose and fell, and it seemed obvious that she was equally content either way.

A final stroke opened a path and the witch banished the rest. It seemed to suck back into her hands and exploded from them in a blizzard of shards. The agent conjured a frost barrier to hide behind but felt the pain when the sharp debris slashed shallow cuts wherever the shield didn't quite stretch. Her legs began to ache from the damage, which suggested serious frost magic had been bound in the attack, but she couldn't spare the time to worry about it. She summoned flame from within and pushed it through her body to warm the affected areas. A quick flick of her fingers launched force darts at her foe.

The witch laughed and raised a hand. The darts struck her flesh and vanished. *Okay, so you have skills. Big deal.* Diana charged, her left hand ready to attack or defend and right hand weaving Fury in threatening arcs. The shadow magic Iressa fired at her spread from its initial point, and she had no chance to avoid it. Instead, she shrouded herself in fire and leapt into the darkness, her momentum more than sufficient to carry her through it for a fatal strike at the woman.

More than sufficient, that is, until the tentacles snaked around her, many more than she'd ever felt. They pushed against her fire cocoon and sought any crevice to sneak through. She thought about the charm at her wrist but rather than invoke it, she followed a whispered suggestion from Fury and raised the blade to touch the tendrils while she restored the thread of lightning and fire she'd used earlier. The appendages recoiled, seemingly in pain themselves. Diana fell to one knee but darted up with the sword in guard position to see Iressa staring at her with her hands on her hips.

Her voice was conversational. "Damn you, Diana Sheen. You have been a thorn in my side for months. A stone in my shoe. A bee in my garden."

Shit. She really is nuts. "Bonnet."

The witch frowned. "What?"

"Bonnet. Bee in your bonnet."

Her adversary wore the same look Nylotte did when Diana had apparently said something so stupid it was literally the most exasperating thing on Earth at that particular moment. Iressa raised a casual hand and a treasure chest was wrenched from the wall and careened toward her head. When she ducked, it continued behind her to crash into the doorway and drew a yelp from Rath.

"Missed me. Would you like to try again? I can move closer."

The witch growled and waved her hands in a complicated pattern that felt all kinds of wrong. Shadow emanated from the artifact tattoos on her left arm—the original one—and lengthened into a long whip. When it finished growing, it burst into controlled flame. The agent took a step back and raised Fury to guard position. Tentacles grew out of the other artifact and twined about themselves until her right arm merged seamlessly into a wicked spike with barbed edges. Diana tried a lightning blast, but the woman raised the disgusting limb and the magic was simply sucked into it.

Nylotte whispered in her mind, "She's continually trying to portal. I can't join the fight without risking her escape. Do you need me?"

She shook her head. "I've got this." Iressa gave her a strange look, and Diana finished, "Uh...I only wanted you to be aware. You know, before I beat you bloody and take you to jail. I've got this."

The witch's laugh sounded unhinged, and the whip flicked out again. Diana lifted Fury to intercept and was stunned when the lash twisted in midair to avoid the block and scored a line of fire down her leg. It seared through her thick pants and the skin beneath and only the heavy leather of her boot was sufficient to protect her flesh. Her moment of distraction allowed her enemy to close and stab the spike at her eye, so she let her wounded leg collapse and rolled away from the attack. A flash in her vision was the prelude to one of Rath's knives as it struck the point on the end of the witch's arm and fell away ineffectually.

The whip danced in again, this time at her face, and she slashed the sword across its path. It recoiled like a snake and struck again, and she jerked her head back in time to keep her eye. She thrust Fury at Iressa, who was barely in range, and the woman blocked with the spike. Diana had expected the blade to cut through and began to grow concerned when it made no impression.

She schooled her face to neutrality when Nylotte stepped out from her invisibility illusion behind the witch and waved her arms in a circle to slowly and quietly summon a portal. The agent stayed in place and accepted another bite from the whip along her blocking arm. The magical weapon sliced easily through the force shield she'd placed around it. The portal began to fill and it was only an instant before her opponent would realize something was amiss. To distract her, she drove forward with a shout, swung the sword past her target and bulldozed her shoulder into the woman's midsection. She buckled, and Diana pushed her back.

The spike stabbed into her upper back and she screamed but continued to shove.

The whip snarled around her throat and she wheezed in pain but kept her legs pumping.

She stopped abruptly, and the witch fell away toward the portal. Tendrils erupted from her artifacts and reached for Diana, but she simply sliced through them and the whip with Fury and offered Iressa no purchase. Her adversary vanished into the darkness and Nylotte immediately banished the portal.

The agent sank to her knees and fumbled for her healing potion. Rath and Nylotte were there in an instant to help her, and it took less than a minute before she was upright and mobile again. She looked her teacher in the eyes. "Thank you. So much. I don't think I really had it."

Both her friends laughed at that one, and the Dark Elf nodded. "No problem."

"Where did you send her?"

They both turned to gaze at the place where the portal had been. "The World in Between. I promised someone I owe that I'd make it hurt. There's nowhere better for that." She turned to her student. "Unless it's living with you. Honestly, I don't know how the troll and the human manage it." The Drow led the way from the room toward the castle proper and proceeded to explain why Diana would be a terrible roommate.

CHAPTER TWENTY-FIVE

C ara moved without seeing the empty warehouse behind the security agency, her mind on the barren plane occupied by the daggers. Angel and Demon were clad in their white and black armor, respectively, and looked like positive and negative versions of the same image. It seemed as if they resembled each other more and more each time she saw them. They were armed with double daggers, logically, and fought at a pace that would challenge her but not put the battle so far out of reach that she wouldn't learn anything from it.

They conversed as they fought, and metal clanged and rang continually as punctuation to their statements. Demon had expounded upon the engagement at the palace. "You would have been better served to use us more."

She blocked a downward strike but couldn't counter because Angel slashed at her face. When she stopped that as well, she spun low to evade the follow-up stroke. "I thought it was a good mix."

"As do I," Angel replied. "Demon is the jealous type. He always wants to be in the thick of things."

Her opposite snorted. "As if you don't." He launched a clever double stab with one blade, feinting outward before he thrust in, then swung the other with a flourish. She picked off the first with her own knife and lifted her foot to punt his wrist to arrest the second. The momentum continued into a pivot and she kicked out with that heel and connected with his chest, and he backed up a few steps. He pointed the dagger at her face. "You'll have to be at the top of your game to defeat Lechnas."

When she was about to ask him for more detail, Angel surged in with a flurry. Cara marched backward, unable to talk as she put her entire being into defending against the quick flicks, stabs, and strikes the sentient dagger thrust at her. Finally, an opening appeared and she leapt forward to bring her leg around parallel to the ground and catch the back of her opponent's knees. The woman in white turned the unbalancing attack into a backflip and her feet landed gracefully on the broken soil.

The agent shook her head in admiration and asked, "What does he mean about Lechnas?"

Angel stepped into a guard position, one dagger held high over her head and pointed like a scorpion's tail and the other forward and low, ready to defend. "He is more dangerous than any three people you have faced so far."

Thinking the avatar might be distracted, she rushed into the attack. A spin brought her left-hand blade around reversed in a stab at her opponent's neck, but she had already mimicked the spin and was no longer there. More by instinct than reason, Cara leapt into the air and avoided the foot sweep that passed under her. She kicked back while still airborne and made contact, then dove and rolled when she landed. Demon appeared from thin air, already in mid-swing, and when she raised her own blades to counter, he turned to smoke and vanished.

It gave Angel time to resume her attack and finally, the agent succumbed as she always did. The daggers returned to their sheaths to signify the end of the session, and she sat on the parched earth. The other two did the same. As if there had been no pause in the conversation, Angel added, "Even more so than Iressa, although you did not battle her."

Cara replied, "Hey, that wasn't my call."

Demon laughed. "That would have been a fight worth watching. She has long been known to us, as her desire to possess Rhazdon's Vengeance began when she was but a child."

The comment jarred her brain off course. "Are you saying that when someone wants the daggers, you're aware of it?"

Angel nodded, "If they are a being of power, yes. It allows us to have a sense of who may one day wield us."

"Did you know about me?"

He raised an elegant eyebrow. "Naturally."

She decided that returning to the important matter might be a better idea than finding out what they'd thought of her before the trial and the bonding. "So...Lechnas. What do you know?"

Angel's head moved slowly from side to side. "He is deceptively dangerous. His hands are in many things. We have seen echoes of them for he, too, covets Rhazdon's Vengeance."

Cara sighed and frowned. "That's exactly what we need. That asshole with the whole Rhazdon set."

Both Demon and Angel looked at her with growing concern. "He has Rhazdon's Defense?"

She nodded. "Diana saw him in it. She barely escaped."

They turned their gazes to one another, and some unspoken communication passed between them. Finally, he sighed. "In that case, wielder, your training must become more strenuous and more serious. Until now, we have brought you along slowly. That will have to stop."

That was slowly? Cara couldn't imagine what that change would look like and really didn't want to find out. She rose to her feet as they did, on guard against whatever new approach they might be about to launch. "So, what does this mean otherwise? I merely need to train more?"

Angel shook her head, and there was a touch of sadness in her tone. "You face a test larger than those that have gone before. Until now, he has been content to work his puppets and allow them to take action against you. But when he turns his full attention to your destruction, you and all your friends will be in the greatest danger you've ever faced. His resources are deep, his abilities deeper, and his desire for power unquenchable."

Without another word, they both attacked, and she had one last thought before her mind became too busy to put ideas together. *Fantastic. It definitely seemed like it was all too easy. This will be much better.*

CHAPTER TWENTY-SIX

Deacon grumbled complaints under his breath as he raided the cabinet in his office. Diana had been adamant that he needed to do the run now, right away, and no, he couldn't wait until nighttime. He wasn't at his best in the daytime. Not even vaguely so. His caffeine intake didn't bring him to optimal energy until after nine at night, and this one o'clock pressure was absolute garbage.

He downed a Coke—blissfully cold from Kayleigh's fridge—and sat in his chair. Once settled, he put the noise-canceling headphones on and turned on the soundtrack from the movie *Inception*, which he'd discovered was the best for disconnecting from the sights and sounds around him. The boss had ordered him to set up their virtual systems for instant demolition and to not tell anyone—not even Kitana, who would seriously be beyond ticked when she found out. Plus, because he'd seeded the defensive arrangements with magic, it meant he couldn't simply type in the code. He had to go in using his powers.

The tech loaded up his tools, pushed the button to lock

the door, and pressed the switch that would force everyone else in the building to use wireless while he took over the fiber connection. The loading screen was like the scene in *The Matrix* where the city rushed up to meet their feet, only it was Pittsburgh and he wasn't nearly as handsome as Keanu Reeves despite wearing the same cool outfit on his avatar. His destination appeared in front of him, and he gave the instructions to change it from a place he was defending to a place he was invading. His own protection programs came online against him. Unlike some coders, he didn't leave backdoors in his work. If he could find them, others would be able to as well.

What he did have, however, was an intimate knowledge of the programming in addition to a blueprint of the target with surveillance information drawn on it. The scene rippled, and the building transformed into a Nazi installation, the security systems became Gestapo and SS soldiers intermingled with ordinary sentries, and his clothes altered to the outfit a resistance fighter might wear. His face would look different to everyone who saw it, sowing confusion among interconnected processes.

The first obstacle was the entrance. Evening had arrived with the changing of the scenery and now, a steady stream of classic German convertible cars pulled up and discharged well-dressed officers, doubtless off to a military ball. The simulations drew from pop culture movie archives, and there were many with that theme. There was no way he would enter that door without a solid disguise, and he didn't have the pieces he needed in storage or enough time to create new ones. He waited until all the attention was on an arrival and darted across the street to the shadows at the side of the building.

A series of windows ran the length of the wall about four feet above his head, and the stonework offered sufficient crevices and protrusions for him to climb up and peer in. He opted to run to the back corner to begin, assuming there would be less chance of his peeping tom activities being discovered there than next to the street. He found cracks for his fingers and pulled himself up while his shoes scrabbled to find footholds, and peered inside. Couples were dancing, the women in colorful party dresses twirled by men in uniform. *Okay, not that one.*

Deacon ran in a crouch to the back of the house and repeated the process with one of the windows in the middle and peeked into a small prep room off the kitchen. He was about to climb up when loud voices froze him. A butler and chef walked into the area, leaned against the wall, and lit cigarettes. *Dammit. Okay, I need a different plan.* An option presented itself a few feet farther on where two doors with a simple padlock covered what could only be stairs down to the basement.

Defeating the outer layer of security took only seconds. In the real world, his body pressed the proper buttons to flag the vulnerability for a closer examination after his task was done. It might be something an enemy who tried to hack their network wouldn't see, an artifact of his strange current position as an attacker with extra privileges since it was his own system. But if it was visible to outsiders, that needed attention.

The basement door was accessed equally quickly, and he slipped into the darkened space. The floor was rough concrete with a coating of dirt. Shallow shelves filled with mason jars covered the outer walls. *Okay, I'm into the storage backups. This is a good place to start.* He removed the backpack and placed it on a utility sink in the corner before he extracted several movie-style bombs—red dynamite, black wires, and an oversized analog clock on the front. The backpack contained far more of them than could ever actually fit in a real one and he placed them liberally throughout the room, shoving them anywhere the darkness was sufficient to keep them hidden. None were active and they would remain inert until Diana ordered him to kill the system, at which time they would all activate at once and detonate seconds later.

A staircase led to the first floor. He crept up on soft feet and carefully transferred his weight from one to the next in case of a squeaky board. When he reached the top, he put his ear to the door. Sounds of conversation were audible, and he realized it was the two smokers he'd seen previously. They chatted amiably in a language he couldn't understand and said what sounded like goodbyes before their voices receded. He cracked the door slightly and peered in both directions before he emerged quickly into the room and hurried to a corner out of sight of the entrances. More bombs vanished into storage cabinets, this time tucked away among china and serving pieces. *Heh. That'll make a mess.* The items represented the user side of the system—interfaces, profiles, and the like.

Deacon pushed his sleeve up and looked at the blueprint drawn in marker on his arm. While he would plant explosives when opportunities presented themselves along the way, his main target was the office safe on the second floor, which was the core where the most vital information lived. He remained convinced that an intruder would have almost no chance to access it given the security in place, but he had an advantage. Since he was the architect of the system's defenses, he knew the timing of the guard patrols and could easily avoid them.

It was the autonomous defense programs—the Gestapo and SS officers—that would be the challenge. He moved to the small doorway at the edge of the room and slipped through it into the servants' sleeping quarters. It resembled a military barracks more than anything, with bunk beds and trunks. No one was present as everyone worked during an event this big.

The tech opened one of the chests and withdrew a server's attire. A covered tray from an earlier meal served as a hiding place for the explosives, and a moment of adjustment changed his face from that of a dirty resistance fighter to a prim and proper waiter. He exited into the servant's corridor that ran concealed through the house and finally emerged from the door nearest the steps. A bottle of champagne stood nearby so he took it and continued up the elegant staircase at a measured, dignified pace. When he reached the top, a boisterous man in the black uniform of the SS stopped him and gave him a hard stare before he laughed and extended his glass.

He filled it and departed with a nod. His destination was directly ahead, but the two guards who were always outside posed a problem. However, because he was the architect, he knew where things were. He strode past the sentinels without acknowledging them and moved from one cluster of revelers to another, refilled drinks, and endured enough condescending looks that he wanted to smack the next person to bestow one upon him with the now empty bottle.

Deacon walked around a corner and out of sight of it all and hurried forward into the guards' barracks. This room had triple bunks but also a card table and a large radio. Two patrollers—presumably stationed for emergency response—bolted up in alarm. He drew the suppressed pistol from the back of his waistband and shot them both in the forehead. His breath held, he listened carefully but the system did not respond as if it had noticed, which meant he'd successfully quarantined the outgoing warning. *Damn, I'm good.* After a hasty change of uniform, he stared at one of the downed men and altered his avatar's features to match.

After one final tug at the tunic, he emerged and strode to the guards outside the secure room. He nodded to them and they returned the gesture. When he reached toward the handle, one asked, "Orders?" *Dammit. I guess that would have been too easy.* With a smile, he raised his hand in a small wave. "You do not need to see my orders."

The man turned to the other. "We don't need to see his orders."

It took a little effort to force his face to stillness to hide his grin. He loved being a cyber-Jedi. "I'm merely going about my business."

The second guard nodded. "Go about your business."

The tech entered quickly. The back portion of the office was isolated by a metal wall but he knew the combination. He pulled the creaky door open as slowly as he could and stepped through to conceal more explosives wherever they wouldn't be visible to a casual glance. When he was finished, he considered logging out but feared it might tweak something in the system and make it take notice. Instead, he walked out of the room as merely another guard who patrolled to protect the bigwigs at the party.

He had a moment of shock when a man grasped his arm. "Fraulein Bridget von Hammersmark will be here momentarily. See that the driveway is cleared for her. Oh, and ensure that there is a bottle of champagne waiting." He nodded solemnly and smiled as he walked away. The system's choice of the Tarantino character to represent Kayleigh was inspired, but it meant he needed to leave that much quicker if she were logging in. He stepped out the doors, turned the corner of the house, and kicked the kill switch. *Auf Wiedersehen, Nazi bastards. Score one for the Allies.*

CHAPTER TWENTY-SEVEN

Diana was almost the last to arrive. She hadn't timed it that way intentionally but coordinating one final time with Bryant had taken longer than expected. The restaurant was crowded but then again, it always was. Primanti's was a Pittsburgh icon, the place where they put the fries and coleslaw on the sandwich, making it virtually impossible to fit it into one's mouth. She'd miss it if it became necessary to invoke Project Adonis.

A wave at the bartender as she passed brought her one in return, and she entered the back room that had been reserved for her team with Cara at her heels. Having this particular meeting there seemed appropriate somehow—like a testimony to their time in the city or maybe a farewell. *Okay, enough being maudlin. It's entirely possible we won't need to go anywhere, so quit whining about it.*

Appropriately and true to form, the rest of the team hadn't waited for their leader and had simply ordered and dug in. As she surveyed the scene, a French fry arced to catch Hank in the ear. He looked around for the culprit but none was obvious, so he merely shook his head and returned to his meal. She knew the look on Rath's face well, though, and noted the way his fingers already reached for another missile.

She pressed the button to activate her jammer and stepped to the empty place at the front of the table. Since the room was windowless, they wouldn't have to worry about drones peeking in, which was one of the reasons she'd selected the location. "All right people, I'll make this a quick briefing and we can enjoy ourselves a little." Cara had agreed to stay alcohol-free with her for the night so the others could have a drink if they wanted one, but everyone knew they were now on the job until told otherwise, so no one would overindulge. *Except maybe in giant sandwiches.* They turned their heads her way at least, which was enough.

"First, Lady Alayne is fine and the palace is being repaired. Other kemanas have sent volunteers to supplement her guard force until she can build it up again, hopefully bigger than it was before." Nods were offered in response. "Most importantly, there were no friendly injuries requiring a hospital stay." That comment drew a few laughs and she glared at them, especially Tony.

"Second, we've heard a fair amount about Lechnas, and all of it is bad. Cara?"

Her second in command stepped forward and, probably unconsciously, patted her thighs where the daggers were sheathed when she didn't carry them concealed at her lower back. "Angel and Demon tell me that he is basically flat-out awful—a classic megalomaniac whose whole goal in life is to acquire power and use it for his own benefit.

They also say he's three times as dangerous as anyone we've faced so far."

Tony yelled, "Well, those daggers haven't met me yet," and puffed his chest out. He raised his chin to a regal, heroic pose.

Kayleigh snorted. "Twelve times as dangerous as you, unless we're discussing your unique power of shattering eardrums with Karaoke. There, you've probably won." Laughter greeted her words and Diana shook her head. She'd stayed away from those particular gatherings. There were some things you simply didn't want to know about your coworkers.

Cara gave a thin smile but didn't share the merriment. "Anyway, he'll be a difficult enemy. Plus, he has Rhazdon's Defense, a collection of artifacts that have somehow agreed or been forced to work together."

Diana took over. "Lechnas is our focus now. Nylotte is working on getting us more information on him, but he's apparently extremely secretive and really good at pulling the strings behind the scenes. The whole mess with the Remembrance was ultimately his doing, albeit through a couple of pawns. Plus, he's pressured all the kemanas to submit to his guidance."

Hank raised his hand and she rolled her eyes at the school-like gesture. "Yes, Hank?"

"What's his play? If he wants the kemanas to fall in line, why wasn't he around for that attack?"

"That's a good question and I wish I had an answer for it. Maybe he wanted to see what Iressa was capable of or maybe he was busy with some other evil plot. Those are the best-case answers. Worst case, it's because he's working on something much bigger—which at this point would mean he's targeted us or plans to attack above-ground like he's threatened to do in the past." The kemanas had been given clear warnings that if they didn't submit, both the underground cities and the ones that helped them above the surface would pay the price.

Deacon shouted, "It sounds ugly. What's the plan?"

She nodded. "We'll work on two fronts. First, we need to prepare for the possibility of an attack somewhere in the city and be ready to defend against it when it comes. It's possible he'll go after Stonesreach again but as Hank mentioned, it doesn't make much sense to separate those attacks. So the more likely scenario is up here. We'll loop in the local authorities, military, and whoever we can but ultimately, we can respond fastest and hardest, so we'll be the tip of the spear if that happens.

"But there's another possibility." She punched her right fist lightly into her left palm at sternum height. "It's entirely likely we've pissed him off enough that he'll come for us, directly or as part of an attack on the city. While we here in BAM Pittsburgh have been fairly secure, minus one or two small episodes—*like getting ambushed in a damn restaurant by a horde of enemies*—ARES' oversight committee has been seriously compromised. There's intel out there about us. Add in the ongoing political nonsense that could endanger the organization further, and it all starts to seem like a concerted effort directed at us. Well, us and ARES DC."

Diana shrugged and leaned on the table with both hands. "I'd love for this to be the part where I say something inspirational, but I have nothing. We need to be ready, and when he shows up, we need to kick his ass. Normally, that's where it would end, but I have a bad feeling, Bryant has a bad feeling, and I bet some of you do too." Most of the team nodded except Rath, who continued to eat and Deacon, who stared at the troll, apparently fascinated by his efforts to conquer the huge sandwich.

"But, like any government agency, there are plans for everything, and we have one for basically being screwed by our own side's inability to keep secrets." She straightened again. "It may require us to pick up and go, fast. Thanks to Cara's constant whining and Hank's amazing skills, we now own a mobile armory to do it in. You should all have go-bags ready at home and at the base. If we do have to scramble, we can portal back for anything later, so only pack the essentials and the things you absolutely couldn't bear to lose."

Kayleigh asked, "Is this a permanent thing?"

Diana shook her head. "There is honestly no way to know. If we need to do it, all bets are off and all vacations canceled."

Rath, who'd seen *Spaceballs* for the first and second times the night before since he demanded to watch it again immediately added, "Prepare for ludicrous speed."

Everyone laughed, and she said, "Exactly right. Bryant is briefing his folks too because we're not sure if it's only us or all of ARES that's in danger." She paused for a moment to collect her thoughts before she finished, "And that's all I have. Something's bound to break, and when it does, it'll be fast. It's up to us to be ready for it so we can take whatever happens and shove it down that bastard Lechnas' throat until he chokes on it."

CHAPTER TWENTY-EIGHT

W hen the attack began, the first move was subtle. If Deacon hadn't already been inside the system magically, it might have gone unnoticed. The firewall was constantly tested by everything imaginable from random spam barrages to sophisticated denial of service attacks and all things in between. The AIs were the best security programs he knew of, but Skynet-level technology was still a way off, so they hadn't learned to adapt to everything.

While they were distracted with a big attack, a tiny one snuck in, masquerading as a damaged but unthreatening piece of code. It evaded the initial line of defense and began to burrow into the system. If the enemy had been willing to wait, it might have eventually found a position from which to monitor everything without anyone being aware of it. But the intruder was in a hurry, and like a spider at the center of its web, the tech felt the tremors of its passage.

He'd barely exited the Air National Guard's system

after he'd verified that the gate he'd built into it was still active. It was part of his weekly routine and merely a gentle test that wouldn't be noticed. When he wasn't in a specific simulation, the computer network was like a crowded solar system with planets he could fly to at will. He struck his Superman pose, rushed to the area where the intruder had last been seen, and landed behind the cover of a tree that looked down on a figure who seemed to be writing in a notebook at a distance of about two hundred yards. *Data thief. Bastard.*

He recognized the avatar and bit off a curse. *I killed you once already. Don't you have the sense to stay dead?* The man's white leather armor was pristine enough to reflect the light and today, he had two longswords sheathed at his back instead of the one he'd carried before. His first impulse was to taunt the man before killing him in simulated hand-to-hand, but the wiser part of his brain suggested that even a minimal risk was too much. Instead, he gestured with his hand and two German shepherds appeared and immediately raced along the trail the intruder had left on his way in. The guard dogs would sniff him out and lock the connection open, which in turn would prevent him from fleeing by any means other than a full disconnect.

A case materialized beside the tech and he removed a sniper rifle from it. The Remington M24 was as effective in the virtual space as it was in the real world, and his came loaded with five rounds in its internal magazine. He stretched in the prone position and positioned the weapon before him, the ranging information already present in his head. *Home turf has its advantages.* Once he'd sighted on the man's knee, he squeezed the trigger. The bullet struck its target and he fell. He worked the bolt and aimed again but missed when his prey rolled away. The third shot disabled the man's other leg.

A snap banished the weapon and case, and the tech vaulted from one location to the other and landed in a superhero pose merely for the fun of it. He walked over and used his foot to push his foe onto his back, then yanked off the intruder's mask to reveal a mannequin's skull with only the eyes alive. "Hey, how's that cubicle treating you?"

"At least I'm safe, which is more than I can say for you."

With something close to a smirk on his face, he shook his head. "You really need to work on your threat game. I honestly don't feel it."

A laugh emerged from the frozen mouth. "Perhaps you've not paid close enough attention." The smug certainty in his voice shivered cracks in the foundation of Deacon's confidence. He tuned out for a moment and dispatched a diagnostic request to the AIs. All the team's customized assistants were present in the network, and their semi-autonomy made them superior to routine-based defense code. Harley returned with a response first. "Tunnel through firewall detected."

Deacon conjured a pistol from the air, shot the figure before him, and severed his connection to the system. His foe vanished but he was already looking away and strode toward a huge array of virtual monitors that had risen from the ground behind him. "Show me."

The hole in his security materialized. It resembled a straw from which a thin trickle of red liquid poured, then split, then split again, on and on. The infection was spreading fast. "Quarantine."

The AIs spoke over one another in response to that high-level command and their different personalities rendered all the comments unintelligible. He wouldn't have listened anyway with his full attention on the displays in front of him. The spread slowed, then reversed as the systems pushed back against it. There was nothing he could do about whatever information had already been taken but he could at least ensure no more got out. He pressed the right buttons to send a prepared message to Kayleigh, who was in the lab next door.

A long time later—but what was probably only a minute in the real world—her gaming avatar materialized beside him. "The system is cut off from external inputs and outputs. The version in the mobile armory is running things now. What happened?"

He gestured at the screens. "I'm not sure how the bastards got in, but they did. Are you positive we're secure?"

She nodded. "Yep."

"Okay then, I'll work on cracking the programs they left behind. It doesn't matter if they get farther in since they won't have a connection to take the information anywhere. Maybe I'll learn something. I'll disable the backup process and reload an older version later."

"How will you be sure they aren't in that copy, lying in wait?"

"We can't be sure of anything, at this point." He shrugged. "But if I'm able to find their footprints, we'll know what to look for later."

Kayleigh patted him on the shoulder. "If anyone can do it, it's you. Hack on, my friend."

Gwen's unexpected, "Manny is calling," caused Rath's throw to miss the bullseye and it caught at the edge of the next ring instead. He growled, which drew a chuckle from Chan.

"Put him on, Gwen."

The old man's voice was scratchy, a combination of age and the quality of the connection wherever he was. "Rath?"

"Yep."

"This is Manny."

He stifled a laugh. "Yep. Whatcha need?"

"Charlotte wants to have a chat with you as soon as possible. Well, all of us together. Can you come over?" Their decision to return to the house hadn't been one the troll supported, but he'd learned that once the group set their minds to something, ordinary concerns like danger or reality gained little traction.

"Standby." He looked at Chan. "Work calls. Okay?"

His teacher nodded and seemed satisfied that his student had observed the appropriate formalities in asking. "Of course."

The troll made some hasty calculations. "Can be there in twenty minutes. Good?"

"Great. See you then."

The connection dropped, and he shook his head as he collected the knives from the target and stowed them in his backpack with the batons. His destination was across the university areas from his training garage, so the magical subway was the fastest route. He waved to Chan and ran toward the nearest Starbucks.

The scene in the dining room was much improved since the previous time. There were only three of them there—the man with the long beard, Manny, and Charlotte. He clambered onto the open chair. "Hiya."

They all smiled, and Professor Charlotte spoke as she pushed a cup of tea over to him. "Thanks for coming, Rath."

He sipped the tea, which tasted of cinnamon, a flavor he adored. "Trouble?"

The bearded man had an unexpectedly soft voice, given his overall rough look. "Not for us but maybe for you."

He inclined his head in a question, and Manny picked the discussion up. "There's not all that much action-wise that we can accomplish these days, but you'd be amazed how invisible old folks like us are in a crowd. This means we overhear many things that might otherwise stay secret."

Charlotte nodded. "And the other day, on campus, I heard something troubling from one of the folks we've been worried about." The club that honored the memory of the Silver Griffins had conceived the idea that a university would be a likely place for troublemakers to be and had immediately begun to look for some. Most of their suspects proved to be good people who talked big or had strange interests or both. But a couple seemed like they might really be believers in Rhazdon's message based on their words and their activities, and the group had committed to keeping an eye on them.

"What?"

"Something big is coming."

He nodded. "We're waiting for it. Above-ground this time." He'd shared the tale of the battle in the kemana with them and had seen their burning desire to be a part of making the world better in the way they hung on every word.

She shook her head. "Tonight. It's coming tonight."

Rath's eyes widened. "How know?"

The man with the beard answered. "I tailed him. He went home, packed his belongings, and hightailed it to the bus station. I was behind him when he spoke to a girl who waited for the same ride. Our boy said, 'It's a good time to get out of town. I wouldn't want to be anywhere near the universities tonight.' It's fairly obvious when you put the pieces together, right?"

The troll nodded slowly. He couldn't fault their logic and although their source wasn't the best, it was more than they currently had. He jumped to the floor. "Thank you. For everything. Find a safe place to hide. Somewhere they don't know. Somewhere not here. Please?"

They agreed and seemed struck by the seriousness in his voice. "Take care of yourselves, friends. See you on the flip side." He dashed out the door and contacted Diana to share the news. Seconds later, the base AI, Alfred, instructed all ARES personnel to report to headquarters. Rath shook his head. *Quick stop, first.*

There was no time for subtlety. While he would have liked to follow the communication directions he'd been given, he couldn't wait. When he reached the graveyard, he ran directly to the mausoleum. The front door was locked but there was an ornamental window high up. Rath climbed to it, broke the glass with his elbow, and dropped inside. He grew to his eight-foot form and jumped up and down to make as much noise as possible.

It took only a moment before Amadeo's voice crackled in his comm, cloaked in its usual disguise. "I thought we had an understanding, troll."

"No time. Big attack tonight. Lechnas."

"That bloody bastard. He's dangerous."

"Yes. Know. Need favor."

The assassin laughed. "Haven't I done enough for you already?"

The troll nodded, even though the other man couldn't see it. *Unless he has cameras. He probably has cameras.* "Still. Need it. Will owe you."

"Assuming you survive."

"No doubt. Am Spider-troll. Always survive."

"Okay. You'll owe me and with severe penalties for not paying, right?"

He'd give whatever was necessary without a regret. "Right. Yes. As long as it doesn't hurt my friends or innocents."

"You know my rules. That could have gone unsaid. What do you need?"

"Watch over the Griffins tonight and after if I can't."

Amadeo laughed again but it was less mirthful and more strained, even with the added distortion. "That's a big ask. I'll watch over them tonight and whenever I'm in the city for another reason."

"Deal. Thank you."

"Stay safe, troll. I want my favor repaid."

He grinned, already almost out of the building to take another ride on the subway. "Guaranteed."

CHAPTER TWENTY-NINE

Diana had headed directly to the kemana to ensure that they were prepared for anything that might happen on their side and cursed extravagantly about the uselessness of one-way telepathy. Her parting words had been, "Take the truck and try not to wreck it. It's brand new— like your Arch was." Cara still sputtered a reply when the boss vanished and spent a moment mourning her lost and once incredibly cool motorcycle. In a moment, though, she brushed it off and set to work.

Half the team was present with the others still en route. They knew what to do without her hovering over them, so she climbed the stairs to the labs. Both techs looked stressed while they shoved things into crates customized for the under-floor lockers in the mobile armory. "What can I do?"

Kayleigh shook her head. "Take one of the closed ones and haul it downstairs. Otherwise, nothing for us." The stress of being sent into the field, even though it was only in the truck, was evident in her voice.

Cara lifted two of the heavy crates and found a balance after a slight wobble. "We're out of here in fifteen. Anything that's not packed doesn't go. That doesn't include you two, as I'll have Hank carry you out if necessary. Got it?"

Deacon paused to salute and quipped, "Aye, aye, Commodore Binot," and returned to packing computer gear into boxes, separating the layers with foam inserts while he muttered constantly at a level too low for her to hear.

She lugged the boxes to the bottom floor and threw them on a partly filled metal cart. Anik pushed a fully laden one toward the elevator. She called up the phone interface in her glasses and dialed the front desk of the coworking company in the building above. The security guard answered with a pleasant greeting and she gave him the code phrase that was written in big letters on a sign under the counter of the desk. "Full stop. Evacuate. Keep main doors clear. Execute."

He snapped, "Affirmative," and the line dropped.

Overhead, the renters, workers, staff, guests, and baristas would begin to flow out of the building through one of the three exits other than the main one. "Harley, front door cam." The AI put it on the right side of her vision and she saw the truck pull onto the sidewalk. The elevator doors closed on Anik and she pointed at Tony. "Take it, then help Anik unload his and send him back."

While the armory was fully self-sufficient, the possibility of activating ludicrous speed—to use Rath's term for their exodus—required a little more in the way of supplies. Go-bags had been the first items on the cart, followed by extra magic deflectors. After that, stocks of everything they regularly used—like ammunition, grenades, medical stores, plus some rarities like climbing harnesses in case they needed to do an aerial pickup or deployment—were included. There hadn't been time to build a checklist of what they might need over and above the weapons and equipment usually stored in the van, so it was on her to make sure they didn't forget anything vital.

"Seven and a half minutes. Get a move on," Harley told her and she shook her head. Time was flying faster than usual. She raced up the stairs for another crate. Hank appeared a moment later to help and soon, they had everything loaded into the truck. The large man took his place in the cab and Deacon climbed in beside him. Cara ran to the back and counted heads. "Stark, Khan, Face, Glam"— Rath darted between her legs and onto the bench —"Rambo, and Croft. Only Boss is missing, so we're good."

She tapped her comm. "Alfred, this is Binot. Verify my voiceprint."

His elegant voice answered, "Verified."

"Accept command Full Lockdown."

"Command accepted. Initiating sequence." Inside headquarters, heavy steel doors would descend at most key locations in the ARES portions of the building. At the security agency, they would deploy behind the front entrance and the loading dock. After thirty seconds, the AI reported, "Lockdown confirmed."

She looked at her team. They were calm and prepared as they waited for her order. With a sense of excitement she couldn't deny and wouldn't analyze, she gave it. "Gear up, people. Hank, take us somewhere between the universities." The heavy vehicle lurched into motion.

Kayleigh had donned her haptic gloves and now issued orders through a keyboard that was only visible in her glasses. Voice commands were impossible to use privately in the crowded space, so she typed the things she didn't want the others to hear. *Alfred, connect to Deacon's display, text mode.*

He replied on the private channel in her comm, "Connected."

She typed, *Deacon. It's time for the thing.*

There was a slight delay before his words appeared letter by letter in her view. *Are you sure?*

Yes. Only for backup.

"It's one-time use, remember." She could almost hear him saying it and a ghost of a smile played on her lips.

Rath caught her eye from the other end of the truck and gave her a thumbs-up. She returned it from her position near the medical bay and continued to work. *I know. But there's no guarantee we'll be in town after so might as well do it now.*

This is your last chance to say no.

Do it. Ace in the hole.

At the Air National Guard base, one of the drones held in standby for liftoff rolled out of the hanger and launched, much to the chagrin of the people in charge. Once it was aloft, its transponder was deactivated and it swooped through obstacles to ensure the radar track was lost. In less

time than it took to blink, Deacon had a launching platform that could remain airborne for hours and also carried
two laser-guided Hellfire missiles that could eliminate
almost anyone who came looking for them.

The nervous feeling in Kayleigh's stomach worsened
when he gave her confirmation that it had been done, but
she set her teeth against it. Best case, the UAV would
return to the base unused. Worst case, it might be the
difference between life and death for those she cared about
—or even innocents who were somehow dragged into the
action. Either way, she knew herself well enough to understand that if she didn't do all she could, she'd kick herself
for it forever.

Whatever it takes, I'm all in.

Cara noticed the look on the tech's face but assumed it was
probably nervousness. She wondered for a second if she
should ask her about it but decided it wouldn't be awesome
to call her out in front of everyone. A quick scrutiny down
the line revealed that the rest of the team was perhaps
halfway prepared. The clock and map in her display
claimed they were about six minutes from their destination, so there was time and it was unlikely things would
kick off the instant they arrived anyway.

She stored a concern with each item she put on over
the boots, pants, and tunic she already wore. Worry about
her own survival faded as the uniform shirt came on,
pushed further into the distance with each button. The
heavy utility belt clicked into place and banished her fear

that someone on her team would be hurt. She wouldn't let that happen. Fastening the Velcro on her vest helped her store her biggest worry—that she'd somehow fail her comrades—in the box where she kept it on the rare occasions it emerged. She never had, not in anything important, and she certainly wasn't about to start tonight.

With her gear in place, she moved to the rack of grenades and distributed sonics and flashbangs since they didn't know whether there would be civilians in the fight zone. She withdrew magazines from their storage and handed them down the line until everyone had a full load of anti-magic bullets for both pistol and carbine. No one asked for revolver rounds, so she assumed the backup weapons were properly prepared. Hers was at all times, and her team most likely operated on the same ethic.

The ARES second in command stood and studied her people with a deep sense of pride. She kept her face neutral so they wouldn't see how much she admired their dedication, professionalism, and bravery. Tony gave her a grin that told her she hadn't fooled anyone. Before he could say anything to ruin the moment, the truck stopped abruptly and rocked on its shocks.

"We're here," Hank reported. "What's the plan?"

She laughed. "What's always the plan? Hurry up and wait, and when the bug sticks its head out of its hidey-hole, we crush it."

Diana downshifted as she threw the Charger into a tight turn and accelerated. As much as she didn't want to take her own car to a potential fight scene, she also didn't want to detour to the base when her house was closer. She honked and wove through traffic, hoping there weren't any black-and-whites on her route. Her glasses displayed the route to where the truck was parked, a couple of blocks away from the main parts of the two campuses. She had to admit it was a solid choice to create maximum damage in a confined space. All those students in class and clustered in such a small area. *That is so not good.*

A student thought about stepping off the curb as she accelerated toward him and she flicked her fingers to push him away from the street. He was a surprised blur as she rocketed past and she laughed at the image. She pulled in far enough away from the truck that she wouldn't be in the way of any maneuvers and high-fived Hank as he opened the doors for her to climb inside. Cara stood beside the pistols and greeted her with a fist-bump.

"Damn fine job, people." She studied her team quickly and nodded. "You look like you're ready to kick serious ass."

Tony replied, "You look like you're ready to go to a heavy metal concert."

She sighed. "Listen, I like to drive with my windows open, my hair was wet, and by the way, bite me, you Yosemite-Sam-looking jagoff." The comedy routine had the desired effect and the moderate tension in the room vanished under laughter. She pulled off her casual clothes and donned her uniform, handing Fury to Cara while she changed. When the sheathed blade slipped through the loops on the back of her vest, everything felt perfect.

The team waited in silence, each tuned to their own

pre-battle process. A sense of finality and of many threads of fate coming together at a single point hung in the air. When darkness fell, they'd been in the vehicle for a little over ninety minutes.

Finally, in a voice that sounded half-scared and half-excited, Deacon announced, "Contact."

CHAPTER THIRTY

K ayleigh took over as technological interface for the team after her colleague's announcement. "Okay, let's see what we have here." She monitored the feeds from the watchers, saw what Deacon had referred to, and threw it into the agents' displays. Her frown deepened as she accessed the drone and brought it lower for a better look and manipulated an invisible flight stick with the sensors in her gloves. What looked like two dozen Kilomea, along with half that number of wizards and witches, marched in a diamond formation down the main street that connected the two universities. They'd ignored the one farther to the east, which meant they had targeted the one closer to downtown with the high tower that held Rath's gear.

After a vivid flash, the feed went dark. She rewound the video and saw that a wizard had blasted the mechanical with lightning. "Dammit. Routing more watchers in. I'll keep them higher."

Diana wasted no time. "Let's go people." There was a

great deal of banging from her left and chatter on the headsets, but Kayleigh remained focused.

"Deacon, see if you can strafe them with a stun drone from the rear."

"On it."

She tagged the lead person in the formation and slaved the incoming watcher to it, then acquired her own stun drone and piloted it toward the scene. Her display showed that her timing didn't match the other tech's, so she had him circle once to compensate. The two rushed in together, fired at max range, and continued to discharge stun blasts as they closed.

For a second, it seemed like it would work but shields appeared at the front and back to block the assaults. Other wands raised and soon, the feeds from those drones dropped as well. She pounded her leg with a fist and yelled, "These damn bastards suck."

Deacon's voice was calm but angry. "Okay, sure. They knew to look for drones. So what we need to do is put them in ambush positions..." He trailed off before he finished.

"Deacon?"

"Uh...you definitely won't like this. I left a tracing program active in case that signal came back—the one from Diana's fake text."

"And?"

"And it has arrived. There are drones on the way."

Kayleigh toggled her mic on in the group channel, which had been full of the team rushing to find positions to intercept the marching Kilomea. "Boss, we have a problem. There are enemy drones inbound."

Diana cursed and said the worst words ever. "You two have to take care of it. We need to deal with these on the ground since they are destroying your stun drones. Fight well, Glam."

Her mouth stayed open for five seconds while she processed the order before she shut it with a snap. "Okay, so it's on us."

He laughed. "I heard. Of course it is."

She nodded, even though he couldn't see her. "Okay. We have watchers galore and a few more stun drones. Let's try one of those. Can you give me a target?" A map appeared with a red dot on it and she used the virtual flight stick to steer one of the watchers onto it. "Okay, these things weren't made to track fast objects, so we'll have to go manual. How about a crosshair?"

"Geez, Kitana, you don't ask for much, do you?" He growled his irritation. "Reprogram a damn drone on the fly while doing seven other tasks. Sure. Hang on." He went silent for a while, and about twenty seconds before her drone would be in range, the crosshair appeared. The weapon was on a fixed mount, so she'd have to be hot on the stick to line the enemy UAV up.

When it arrived, she almost didn't see it. It had a dark skin to match the evening sky and only a glint revealed it. She jerked the drone up and held the trigger down, but the blast missed. With a frustrated mutter, she brought it around as quickly as she could and barely made the turn without hitting a building. The enemy hadn't slowed and continued its flight toward the university. An image was frozen in the right-hand corner, and she paled at the sight.

"Deacon, is that what I think it is?"

"Yeah, it has two missiles on it. I bet the two that are behind yours do too."

Her display calculated that it would take her drone thirty seconds to reach optimal firing range, so she dropped the designator on the enemy and tapped auto-follow. The local version of Alfred would ensure it stayed on course. Thinking of the AI triggered another idea. "Ralph. Do you have an autonomous defensive mode?"

The low voice answered immediately, "Affirmative."

"Lockouts for friendly forces?"

"Affirmative. ARES, Police, Fire, Military."

She tapped her chin. "Go autonomous but do not fire unless fired upon without direct approval from a member of the ARES team. If you detect incoming, alert Deacon."

"Affirmative. Autonomous defenses activated."

A whir accompanied the two turrets that slid out from their storage compartments and went through their diagnostics. By then, she was in firing range and she pulled the trigger. The first struck home and her target shuddered but didn't fall. Smoke filled her screen as she fired again, and the enemy vehicle fell away. Two more dots represented the rockets that had been launched.

"Deacon—"

"Quiet, I'm working. I almost have it. There." On the last word, a drone flashed in front of the missiles, fell victim to the first, and created a fireball that consumed the second. She released the breath she'd held.

"That was close."

"So are the other two."

Kayleigh flicked through the available toys and found another nearby watcher. It didn't have any weapons but that was okay. Deacon had given her the solution. She grinned as the enemy grew large in her display when she streaked toward it from above and the picture died when the drones collided and fell in a smoking heap.

She leaned back and wiped her sweaty forehead to watch her fellow tech repeat the process with the other enemy mechanical. She breathed a sigh of relief and called up the cameras observing the field team.

Cara crouched about a block down from the advancing ranks and around the corner of a large building. Hank and Anik stood behind her, and all three had their rifles in hand and waited for the enemy to move into range. She'd considered heading to the roof but they hadn't brought any climbing gear and she couldn't fake-fly the way Diana did.

Across the four-lane street, the boss held a similar position with Tony on her six. Sloan and Rath were a half-block farther away from the oncoming attackers, ready to take potshots where they could. The team's face wasn't as effective in close combat as the others and Diana wanted to keep the troll out of the initial battle since guns would work far better than knives.

No one had argued, least of all her. If the boss was aware that she and Anik were an item, she hadn't mentioned it and she always worked well with Hank. *Everyone knows this.* Plus, Diana's superior magic skills would make up for having fewer people on her team. The idea of an in-house fight club—suggested once by Hank— had taken hold in her mind, and going up against the other woman's impressive abilities was one of the things she would enjoy trying. *In a controlled environment with rules and pads and healing potions.*

The boss' voice was soft and low. "Wait until they're close. Wizards and witches first. Hose the Kilomea down, then aim at joints and heads. The anti-magic rounds are iffy on them."

Hank chuckled. "This is one more time we could have used AP, Boss."

"Yeah, where a ricochet could ruin a civilian's day. Nah, we'll do it the hard way."

"That's good, I like it hard," Cara quipped.

The channel filled with soft laughter and Diana ordered, "Quiet, people. Stand by. Moving in three, two…" At zero, they stepped out from behind cover. A cry went up when the enemy saw them, but fingers had already tightened on triggers and they immediately delivered a volley at the wizards and witches in the front. Those targeted conjured shields that did them no good and fell in the initial salvo. The Kilomea, like the experienced warriors they were, separated into two halves and then once more. Some on each side attempted to escape the defenders' line of sight to continue their advance while the remainder compelled the shooters to focus on them.

Cara's magazine clicked empty and she released it smoothly to fall near her feet, then retrieved and slotted in the replacement. She fired again a second later. The lead Kilomea absorbed considerable firepower but their thick brown leather armor stopped most of the rounds. Those that punched through or struck exposed flesh looked like they did some damage, but the attack hardly slowed.

"Glam, a little drone support?" Diana yelled. The attackers were about ten seconds away from their positions.

"Negative. Blown up, sir." The movie reference fell flat, although Cara smiled. She'd always had a special love for Bill Murray.

The boss groaned. "Okay, people, stay out of each other's firing lines. Mix it up."

The second in command ran forward, let her gun hang, and drew Angel and Demon. They spoke into her mind to show her the openings she might not have seen herself and warned her of dangers she would now have an opportunity to prepare for rather than react to. She cut a bloody trail through the Kilomea who had barreled ahead and were already compromised after being peppered with bullets. The sound of Hank's booming shotgun caught her attention, and she turned to slice her way to him. By the time she reached the place where she'd left her partners, the hulks on that side were gone.

She looked over to where Diana sliced the last one on her side with Fury, the woman's expression as perplexed as she felt.

"That seemed too easy, didn't it?" Cara asked.

Kayleigh answered. "Attacks coming in from the north and the west. Move it, people."

CHAPTER THIRTY-ONE

While the agents repositioned, Kayleigh viewed the scene from high above through one of the watchers. The two incoming groups were each twice the size of the diversionary force and had already begun their destruction. Several storefronts were aflame and students and pedestrians ran screaming ahead of their advance from both directions. She cursed her inability to make a difference. *Two minutes...what can I do in the next two minutes to help them?*

She routed the images into their displays but could come up with nothing that seemed even remotely viable. Deacon broke her train of thought with a curse. "They're inside the headquarters."

Kayleigh was sure she'd misheard him. "What?"

A window appeared in her glasses and displayed a picture of his office. "I doubled this camera with a cell signal only I can access. I wanted independent verification that no one was messing with my stuff, especially the person in the lab next door." An unknown individual sat at his desk. The long hair and painted nails suggested a female and the way the screens flickered as she attacked the system confirmed magical powers. "Oh, hell—no, you don't." After a short pause, he laughed. "Watch this."

The woman stood suddenly, snatched up the nearest keyboard, and turned and threw it at the security camera. He rewound the image to show her face, which was filled with rage.

"What did you do?" his teammate asked

His voice still retained a distinctly smug edge. "Boss told me to set the system up to self-destruct. I wasn't sure why. Actually, I'm still not sure why. But anyway, I waited until she was close to the thing she was looking for—until she was, like, one lock away—and blew it up."

His coworker looked at the frozen picture. "I guess I can see why that would upset her."

"Right?"

"Diana's gonna be ticked. Even without the information, there's good stuff in there." She summoned the watchers that weren't already on-site and redirected them to the building. *If they use vehicles instead of portals, I'll track them so we can deal with them later.* On the main image in her glasses, the opposing force had started the next phase of their attack.

Diana pounded toward the newcomers, annoyed that they'd thought to create a diversion but not upset that her team had fallen for it. *Diversion or not, those jerks had to be stopped, but it unfortunately allowed these jerks to stay around a little longer.* Ahead, the flow of enemies had branched out to the point where it wasn't clear what their objective was, other than mass chaos and destruction. Kilomea worked in groups of two and three to torment civilians, and wizards and witches seemed giddy over the opportunity to shoot fireballs through the windows of the stores and restaurants that lined the streets. Vehicles also appeared to be a special treat, and deafening explosions echoed from the surrounding buildings as they were shattered by numerous blasts.

She slowed to a jog and focused on the feed from one of the watchers above. "They're splitting up. We'll do the same. Three groups…" Her words trailed off as a tag appeared on a figure made small by the height of the camera. "Stand by. Magnify that image." Her AI complied and she growled with suppressed fury. "Lechnas is here in person. That changes things. Four groups. Stark and Face, make the group to the right as unhappy as you want. Hercules and Khan, you have the ones on the left. Croft, the middle is yours. Rambo and I will target that asswipe."

In response to her words, a path toward the enemy leader appeared in her display. She looked at her partner. "Are you ready for this, buddy?"

He tapped his batons together. "You betcha."

"Then let's get to it."

Tony led the way to the right and aimed for a grassy expanse that bordered two five-story buildings set at an angle to one another. Normally a place where students could sunbathe or throw footballs and baseballs, it now hosted a chaotic race for safety from the madness that had descended upon the university. He jogged as the marauders approached and paused when an opportunity for a headshot presented itself. The enemy hadn't noticed them yet as he'd hunted around the edges, but that wouldn't continue for long.

Sloan asked, "What's the plan, man?"

He squeezed the trigger of his carbine and a lone Kilomea who had moved away from the pack fell. "I'm not sure. This is totally nuts, you know?" A large rock painted in school colors rested nearby, and he dashed over to it. They crouched in its shadow and peered over the top. "We have to eliminate the wizards and witches first. The hulks suck but at least we can run from them if we need to. The magicals, not so much."

His partner laughed. "This really makes me wish I'd taken time to see if I could do other types of magic."

"You'll have your chance." Tony clapped him on the shoulder and pointed at two wizards at the back. "It looks like those two are the rearguard of this group. Let's circle and get rid of them, then keep shooting until someone notices us. We can regroup from there."

Sloan reached position a few moments before he did. They raised their rifles together, dropped the mages with carefully aimed bursts, and raked their fire over the crowd at a Kilomea's head height to ensure they wouldn't hit any innocents. The enemy charge stopped and turned to face them.

Tony hadn't realized exactly how many of the brutes were spread out in the recreational area, but when they came together as a group, it was definitely far more than he'd expected. He caught Sloan's arm and hauled him toward the nearest building. "Good going. I think you made them mad so we'd better get inside." His partner sputtered for a reply but failed to deliver one.

His own laugh faltered when he checked on the Kilomean horde and broke into a run. *Huh. Not only are there more of them than I thought, they're also much faster than they look.*

Hank sprinted toward the group on the left, which had gathered on the plaza and proceeded to wreck everything in sight. The park benches were upended and the islands of greenery ripped out or burning, and the wizards and witches continued to destroy every store they came across. Sirens were audible in the distance. "Glam, warn fire and police that this is an active scene. They might want to stay on the perimeter."

The tech's clipped, "Affirmative. I'm on it," allowed him to put that worry out of his mind. *Only a couple of dozen other things to worry about.* The enemy hadn't noticed them yet, but he and his partner would soon be close enough to fire and once they did, any advantage would be lost.

"Khan, suggestions?"

The man laughed darkly. "Uh...go back in time and rig the plaza to blow up. That's all I have, really."

"Yeah, not helpful but thanks." His mind raced to find a solution, but he couldn't come up with anything clever. "Okay, let's do this. We'll skirt to the right and target the witches and wizards on the outside at the storefronts first. When the Kilomea respond, I'll engage them and you continue with the casters. If we are overwhelmed, we retreat into one of the stores. There's probably a back alley or something connecting them we can use ."

"That's a good plan. I only wish the boss had let us bring real grenades."

He chuckled. "You can't solve every problem by blowing it up, Khan." He crouched and scuttled forward in the cover of the low wall that formed the street-side boundary of the plaza.

"Name one."

It seemed prudent to ignore the challenge. "Stand by. We'll go in three." He counted down and ran up the short flight of stairs to the elevated common area. The nearest witch didn't even have time to notice them before his triple-burst felled her, and Anik repeated the process with the next. Yelling and crashing from the surrounding destruction masked the sound of their weapons, and they were able to kill two more before anyone noticed they were there. The fifth caster, a wizard, conjured a transparent shield but their bullets pierced it without slowing and removed him from the fight as well.

"Uh...Hank, incoming." He turned at Anik's words to face a group of Kilomea that approached from his left. Ahead, the witch who was their next target had summoned a giant hunk of broken concrete to hide behind and twitched her wand to adjust the trajectory of the even larger piece—almost twice his size—that careened toward them.

Adrenaline pumped through Cara as she sprinted to where the two different groups had come together to sow chaos. The student union was aflame and the historic brick building that was one of the most well-known locations on the campus burned fast and hot. Witches and wizards ranged along the front launched fireballs through the windows. She wanted nothing more than to thrust them all inside so they could experience the results of their actions firsthand.

Instead, she stopped, raised her rifle, and mowed them down with a quick triple-burst for each. When they were effectively terminated, she switched magazines and sought new targets. A wealth of options presented themselves—so many that she didn't know where to start. The daggers gave her a nudge and a wizard near the side glowed in her vision. She shot him, engaged their next choice, and moved on to their next. Too cautious to remain in one position for any longer than necessary, she hurried toward the burning building to use its shifting light as cover and claimed another witch casualty on the way.

She found a good position and managed to eliminate one more caster before she was finally noticed. A wizard assaulted the pillar she hid behind with a force blast that cracked it in two, and she had to dive forward to avoid the porch roof above her when it collapsed. She rolled to her feet and wiped the smile from his face with a rifle bullet that caught him in the arm, but her follow-up shot failed when the weapon jammed. She reacted instantly and pounded a fireball into his chest, and he fell.

Suddenly, a bright red light filled the air. She thought, at first, that it was visual smear from her attack, but a glance upward revealed a series of huge scarlet fireworks that exploded and streaked up from the ground near where they'd seen Lechnas. The destruction around her ceased and all the nearby invaders turned in circles, clearly looking for something. When they all stopped and faced her, she realized she was what they had sought.

Uh oh. If this were my plan, that would have been the signal for phase two, which seems like it won't be good for us.

CHAPTER THIRTY-TWO

The red light flickered through the windows while Tony and Sloan crouched on the balcony that ran around the second floor above the lobby. The building's cold war construction and metal doors held up against the Kilomeas' attempts to break in. Despite that, he didn't think the hasty damage they'd done to jam the doors would keep a determined caster out—or even hold up against the current abuse much longer.

Sloan sounded calm but not particularly happy. "Glam, is there another way out of this place if we can't reach the main level?"

There was a pause during which the banging stopped, and the two men exchanged worried glances. Finally, she replied. "It depends. How do you feel about jumping through a window from the second floor?" A map appeared in his vision and displayed a highlighted path. "The good news is there's grass outside the one I've marked."

"Great, thanks—awesome, it couldn't be better. Out." She chuckled at his fast, sarcastic delivery.

The doors buckled like they were under pressure, and a sound between a creak and a squeal echoed through the empty lobby. It cut off when the heavy steel panels careened into the open space and bounced off a column in the middle with a loud clang. Kilomea swarmed in.

Tony said, "Shooting gallery." Both men raised their rifles and fired at anything that moved. He made it through a whole magazine and part of another before the wizard entered and launched a fireball at their position. They both ducked to allow the flames to pass over their heads. He pointed. "Staircase."

They ran in a crouch toward the open quadruple-wide stairs that connected the lobby to the upper floors. Deacon had already hacked the elevators so they couldn't be flanked from that direction, and if they were in truly dire straits, they could use them to escape to a higher floor. The emergency route didn't permit entry on this level, so they'd hear it if the enemy chose to break through that way.

Kilomea marched up the stairs at a deliberate pace, not running but not walking either. There were at least ten and more were visible below and out of easy firing range, seemingly waiting to ensure the others ascended safely. At Tony's nod, both men dropped flash-bangs that rolled down the steps. They detonated directly in front of the advancing line and their rifles chattered as they sprayed the distracted creatures. When their carbines clicked empty, they drew back into cover. A feed from one of the building's security cameras had been added to his display during the action and showed that the first group was half-down and those still mobile were injured.

The duo fell back when a wall of fire appeared at the top of the stairs, a natural reaction to having immobile lava suddenly appear before them, but it soon became a strategic choice when the opposition advanced in safety under its protection. Tony fired three shots as an experiment, and although they penetrated the magical barrier, the angle was all wrong. The camera showed the bulk of the enemy troops still gathered behind it. "Throw the sonics."

Sloan nodded and complied, and as the wall fell, the ordnance soared over the frontmost enemies and clattered down the stairs toward the casters before they detonated. The Kilomea charged in numbers too great for the agents to eliminate them before they were overrun. Tony yelled for a retreat and took the lead and they sprinted along the path to the window Kayleigh had marked. The corridors were narrow and the route involved a considerable number of turns. The pursuers' thirst for vengeance and innate physical prowess allowed them to close the distance quickly, and the agents were only a few seconds ahead when they entered the long corridor with the exit of choice at the end.

"You know they'll follow us out, right?" the Face said over the comm between pants.

Tony nodded. "We'll deal with that when we get there. At least we're still ahead." He shielded his face with his arms as he leapt out the window, followed a moment later by his partner. Once through, he looked for the promised grass. Standing on it was a Kilomea with his head raised. When they made eye contact, the giant grinned.

Okay, so we're not ahead. Bloody hell. He landed beside the creature and rolled to his feet, drew his pistols, and fired at its knees to cover the other man's landing. "Run to the street, we'll regroup in the chaos."

Hank flung himself aside to evade the mammoth block—which was unexpectedly tinted red from something happening above—and hoped Anik had done the same.

"Into the bookstore—now, go!" He barreled toward it and away from the Kilomea. It was one of the storefronts the wizards had already attacked so there were small fires throughout the interior, but the enemies had been cut down before they could turn it into a true conflagration. As he hurdled through the opening where the window had been, he banged into a mannequin dressed in a burning graduation gown. A quick survey for defensible positions revealed no obvious ones. He'd expected bookshelves, at least, but it seemed like actual books were a secondary concern to electronics, magazines, and snacks.

Anik pounded toward the rear of the store and Hank turned to walk backward after him, his rifle trained on the broken windows and door at the front. When Kilomean faces appeared, he released a steady barrage and emptied a magazine before he'd made it more than ten feet. A quick swap and more rounds reduced the incoming horde to half. Wizards peeked around the corner and he released the carbine to hang by its strap before he sailed both of his sonic grenades over the closer enemies' heads. The magicals fell away when the canisters detonated.

The distraction put him in hand-to-hand range. He dimly heard Anik report that he'd opened the back door and discovered a utility corridor, but his mind was occupied with the six giant brutes in front of him. An ax swung viciously and he ducked under it and came up already punching, a swift one-two at normal strength that drove into the attacker's chest and produced sharp cracks when the stun discharge dropped him. The surge of magic within him was pure pleasure, and he stepped inside the next attack—this time a downward chop from a sword—and vaulted to plant his forehead in the Kilomea's nose. The creature recoiled and he punched him in the ribs with three rapid blows, each empowered by shock blasts.

Gunfire sounded and a shout emanated from his left. *Good work, Khan.* The group was clustered so tightly that the long weapons the Kilomea carried put them at a disadvantage. He chopped a hand to the throat of the nearest target and broke his jaw with the hard protrusions on top of his metal knuckles. The burning as a knife dug into his thigh was severe enough to interrupt his next attack, and he stumbled to the side. It ripped out to leave him bleeding, and he staggered back and trusted Anik's rifle to keep the others off him. He retrieved his healing flask and drained it he headed to the rear door. "Let's retreat before the mages get their acts together."

His teammate led the way down the corridor as they sprinted toward the exit at the far end. The sound of heavy feet in pursuit echoed from the tile floors and industrial walls and grew louder and nearer with every step.

Cara uttered a low curse. "Hey, they seem less concerned about breaking stuff and more concerned about breaking me. What's the deal?"

The others responded with variations on the same message, and Diana replied, "Okay, so it's about us. Do you all feel special?" Laughter greeted the quip, but it was tired and didn't burst with confidence. "Keep yourselves safe. If you're able to reach my position easily, do it and we'll engage Lechnas as a group. Otherwise, stay on the move, eliminate targets of opportunity, and don't get caught. Worst case, run to the truck. Glam, any help?"

The frustration level in the tech's voice was more than Cara had ever heard from her. "Nothing. The stun drones are down and the watchers are useless for anything other than...well, watching. And knocking other UAVs out of the sky. Permission to deploy the one from the roof?"

Hank said, "No," before Diana answered, "Denied. We need it to cover our escape if we have to run. That should be an absolute last priority. But you're released to make the call if I'm out of contact."

"Awesome." Kayleigh didn't sound like it was actually awesome at all—the opposite, in fact.

The enemies around Cara were closing slowly, careful to keep her hemmed in. Behind her, the student union burned merrily and the foes in front blocked all her other exit routes. She considered the idea of attempting a fire blast to throw herself through the air the way Diana used force but put it aside. It did, however, spark another thought. She asked the daggers—who had more exposure to magic than she did—and they agreed that it was possible.

Possible is better than being killed here by not trying it. She focused her mind using one of the techniques Nylotte had drilled into her. It wasn't all that complicated but had taken a while to master because thoughts preferred the old habits of making themselves known on their terms.

She pictured the intrusive thoughts bouncing around in her brain and pushed them gently aside, then put police caution tape in front of them to hold them there. After a moment, she was ready and built a second skin of fire an inch from her own, turned, and dove through a shattered window into the burning structure.

It surprised her how well her own flames kept the heat from the others at bay and chose what looked like the safest route through the building. On the far side, the area she could see was mostly empty as the action had progressed beyond it. Two wizards stood outside one of the shattered windows and chatted casually while they launched fireballs into the tall office tower across the street. She wanted to make them bleed but suppressed the desire to challenge them in hand-to-hand combat in favor of banishing her protective skin and delivering a rapid triple-tap in the backs of their heads with her pistol. They fell and she spun away and pounded down the sidewalk toward Diana and Rath.

Kayleigh was sure she was slowly losing her mind. The borrowed UAV circled overhead but was a one-shot tool and she didn't want to get it wrong. The watchers revealed Tony and Sloan racing into the street where cars exploded and enemies targeted anything that moved. A shimmer indicated that a wizard attack was consumed by their deflectors, and they sprinted in a different direction and fired behind them as they moved.

In a separate portion of her visual field, Hank and Anik broke out onto a parallel street one block away and barreled at full speed toward the other two. Cara moved unopposed along another road a block up from the main action. Diana and Rath had stopped, and the chief bastard stood tall a hundred feet beyond them in his fancy armor with a trio of assistants at hand.

As soon as she'd seen him, she'd told Deacon they should take the shot but he had argued against it. She had to admit that it did seem fairly easy, so it might be a trap, and they didn't want to waste their only edge. Instead, she watched and fretted—until his voice, full of alarm, sounded on the channel only they shared.

"Glam. The enemy drone signals are back."

CHAPTER THIRTY-THREE

Cara sprinted into place beside Diana and Rath and her boss quipped, "About time you got here. You need to run more."

The troll laughed. "Must train."

She shook her head but couldn't restrain a smile. "What's the plan?"

Diana shrugged. "Kick his ass back to Oriceran—or into the ground."

Her eye-roll drew a chuckle from her teammates. "Anything more specific?"

"You're so needy. Okay, I'll go engage the leader. You take on two of his friends. Rath, which one do you want?"

"Left."

"Good deal. Be fast but remember that staying alive is key. He's an unknown, and that armor makes everything worse. I can't predict what it might do, but I'm willing to bet the house those damned shadow tentacles will show up. Be careful."

They waited and watched until it appeared that the enemy leader was distracted by something. Their boss breathed deeply. "Go, go, go."

No one hesitated.

———

Diana surged toward the tall figure in the dark medieval-styled armor. She didn't bother with any attempt to shoot at him and had already abandoned her carbine so it wouldn't get in the way. There was enough debris around that he would be able to block easily, and his almost certain magical superiority would make a ranged battle a losing proposition.

Her internal voice manifested for a moment and said, *"It's not that you want to beat him in a way that lets him know who defeated him or anything, right?"* No. Definitely not. Probably not. Shut up.

Her boots coped with the uneven rubble on the street with ease as she drew on the last ounce of speed she possessed. Still, it wasn't fast enough to get there before he noticed her. With a broad grin, he flicked his fingers and a car door rocketed toward her head. She used her telekinesis to deflect it aside slightly and did the same with the tire that followed. He increased the tempo, threw anything and everything not nailed down, and she redirected it all while she continued to close.

His minions—who had initially begun to move toward her—were drawn away by Rath and Cara, which left her target alone. He seemed to grow tired of the game and fired a wide cone of fire and another of shadow at her. The attack expanded to twice her height in a second. Reflex sent her upward and her force blast lifted her over the danger. He banished it as soon as she evaded and waved his arms. She didn't realize his intention until a portal opened farther along her path. She panicked for a moment but her instincts held, and she fired another force blast into a nearby building. The pushback when the sustained power impacted the surface bounced her away from the rift.

Glass rained onto the ground across the street as she skidded to a stop.

"Hello, Diana Sheen," he called out. "It's so nice to see you again. Today, you get the reward you've earned for all your actions against me."

She smirked. "Money is good. You can simply leave it and go. We don't need to be formal about this."

"No, it is you who will bear the cost—you and your people. And it will be high, indeed." He launched a force blast that she dodged but the follow-up beam of shadow struck and consumed several of her deflectors. *Damn. He has serious power. I gotta close before he can do that again.* A ball of fire caught her as she advanced and destroyed the rest of her deflectors but she arrived with Fury drawn and already in a swing. He blocked it with an upraised arm, Rhazdon's Defense against Rhazdon's Vengeance, and seemed surprised when it carved a piece off the armor.

Diana grinned. "Oh, I'm gonna enjoy this."

Watching his friends fight and not being involved had been something akin to torture for Rath. He understood the need, agreed with the concept on a strategic and tactical basis, and hated every second of it. When the moment finally arrived for him to join them, he leapt eagerly to the task.

His target saw him approach and diverted from his original path toward Diana, which was good. He led with fire, which was less good as the widening cone moved faster than he'd expected. There was no way to avoid it completely, but he lurched into a somersault to go through the upper portion rather than through the middle. Deflectors shattered when it connected but he was past it in the next moment and landed in a run and close enough to strike.

Without hesitation, he swung his main hand baton in a vicious arc and aimed at the wizard's head in hopes of ending the fight in a single stroke so he could assist the others. It encountered a force barrier an inch from the man's palm that slowed it so his foe could grasp it. He channeled fire down the weapon and the troll released it and simultaneously struck low with the other one. The man sidestepped to avoid it and made a punching motion. Rath's remaining deflectors shattered and the blowback hurled him onto his rear end. He continued into a roll, found his feet, and ran left to narrowly avoid a shadow blast.

He continued to run in order to draw the man farther from his friends. The wizard pursued and launched more shadow. Rath turned suddenly and threw a knife at his foe's face with his free hand. The mage didn't react quickly enough with his magic but the arm he put in the way saved his vision. The narrow blade stabbed into his flesh and he howled in pain. His smaller adversary charged, and the man waved an arm with a snarl to spread ice along the ground between them. The troll slipped and fell but maintained the presence of mind to toss another knife and reach for a replacement. His blade paused in midair, spun, and retraced its path, now directed at him.

With a low growl, he batted it out of the air with his baton and threw the next, and the process repeated itself. The mage thrust his wand forward, and he had to twist to avoid the thin line of shadow that emerged from it. He finished the twist with another knife in his hand and hurled it sidearm and a little above the ground, hoping the nontraditional attack would fare better than the previous ones.

It sank into his adversary's leg and he fell immediately when the limb folded. Rath found his feet and attacked, using a series of gymnastic moves to avoid shadow tentacles that erupted to stop him. His baton crashed against the caster's wand hand in the same moment that he triggered a spell, and the troll was knocked backward by the force blast. He clambered slowly to his feet, his gaze locked on the wizard, but his enemy didn't move. A closer look revealed that he, too, had taken damage from the misfired magic. The back of his skull was bleeding where it had apparently hit the ground.

Rath shook his head to clear his wobbly vision and turned to find Diana.

She struck down at a diagonal with the sword and aimed at Lechnas' neck. He sidestepped but not quite far enough and she removed another chunk from his armor. Rhazdon's Defense pulsed in her vision as Fury warned her of imminent danger and she conjured a force shield barely in time for it to absorb a wall of shadow that exploded from him. She maintained the protection as she danced in, shifted it aside to swipe at him again, and damaged the metal guarding his leg. He dispatched a second wave of darkness and she waited behind her shield until it had passed before she resumed the attack.

He shifted strategies and rushed forward to meet her. One of his huge gauntlets caught her sword wrist and he drove his helmeted forehead into her face. Her nose broke and brought instant tears, and she ripped her fist free of his grasp and dove to the side in time to avoid the punch from his other metal glove. He pursued and she backpedaled as she rubbed a hand across her eyes to try to clear her vision.

She feinted a further retreat, stabbed forward, and Fury skittered off his armor. She knew what she had to do before the sword told her, even though it would cost her energy. *Well, hell, if I can get a second, I can fix that and the nose too.* She wove fire and lightning into the weapon until the edge sparkled and swung it out to meet the piece of metal he had hurled at her.

The magicked blade sliced through it without effort and the pieces fell to either side of her. Diana nodded. "That's what I'll do to you in your little tin can, asshole."

She thought she saw a trace of worry on his face before the smug half-smile returned.

Lechnas extended an arm and curled his fingers, inviting her to attack. She accepted with a battle cry and charged, certain he had a trap planned for her and aching to turn it back on him.

Cara approached her foes warily after the initial race to draw them away from her boss. The wizard looked old and had a shifty sleaziness she assumed spoke of experience. The witch was young, fierce, and dramatic in her movements, and her burning eyes radiated true belief. The agent wasn't sure she'd ever believed anything that completely, even when she'd been ready to lay her life down for the benefit of her country. Part of her was envious. The other part wanted to show the witch exactly how wrong her beliefs were.

The man attacked first. He twitched his wand forward and a thin cone of lightning erupted from it. She summoned a flame buckler to catch it. The woman spun her wand over her head in a flourish and flicked it at her to dispatch a series of shadow orbs. Another fire shield took care of those. Unfortunately, time worked for the enemy and against her. She'd hoped one of them would make an opening error she could capitalize on, but it didn't look like that would happen. *So, guess I need to mess up their game.*

As they launched the next round of attacks, she sprinted forward and fired darts from both hands at their faces. They looked identical to the full power versions but really weren't, as she'd already expended considerable magic and wanted to conserve what she had left for defense. What they were was an effective distraction, and both her foes halted their assaults to defend themselves. She circled toward the older one, mainly because she assumed the younger caster would be less likely to risk damage to her elder than the other way around. Angel and Demon were eager to get into the fight and crowed happily when she drew them.

He saw her approach and performed an intricate gesture with his wand that trailed a line of fire through the air at neck height. She reacted barely in time, slipped down into a slide, and darted up again once she passed under it. A shadow blast from the witch struck but her deflectors absorbed it and only one was destroyed by the attack. Her adversary tried to dance away from her, but she moved too quickly. She lashed out with Angel and struck her target, and the keen blade sliced through his fashionable boot and severed his Achilles tendon. She came out of the slide, jumped to avoid the burst of flame the woman fired, and sheathed the daggers again as she landed.

The fallen wizard wailed in pain. *Lechnas must have scraped the bottom of the barrel for this group.* She made a slashing gesture and a surge of fire incinerated the wand beside him, which made him howl all the more. His partner attacked with shadow, and she blocked with fire. The follow-up was lightning, and Cara smiled as her flame absorbed it. With each step that closed the distance between them, the woman looked more alarmed and her gestures became sharper and shakier. Ice was consumed by flame. Force was dodged with ease when her foe telegraphed the attack. Finally, she was close enough and Demon pressured her insistently, so she drew the dagger and used its tip to block the witch's next effort. The blade transfixed her wrist and she released her wand and stared at the wound in horror.

Cara spun and delivered a kick that drove her heel into the woman's temple, and she sprawled sideways, unconscious before she landed. As she slid Demon into his sheath, both weapons complained that the fight had been too easy. *Now, where is that big armored scumbag?*

Diana launched a mighty swing aimed at Lechnas's skull. If it had struck, it would have been the decisive blow, but he raised his heavy gauntlet and caught the blade. She fell, her balance broken. She'd seen the shimmer of the force magic, recognized that he'd used the same defense she had before, and cursed herself for not anticipating it.

He reached for the hilt with his other hand, and she growled under her breath, "Oh, hell no." She yanked with her telekinesis but couldn't tear it away from his clutching fingers. Instead, she blasted his hands with waves of force until the weapon was dislodged to clatter onto the street while she scrambled to her feet.

She quick-drew her Glock and fired a stream of bullets at him, but he twitched a twisted car hood in the way and they deflected harmlessly. The distraction gave her a moment to reach out to the sword again, and Fury returned to her hand. She didn't give him time to attack but surged in close. They exchanged attacks and she gouged his armor a few times while he connected with a kick that left her limping.

The two combatants took a moment to study one another. She had begun to think there might not be a way through his defenses, but that at least he hadn't gotten through hers either. Before she could turn her focus to finding a new strategy, a strange buzzing noise reached her ears. The enemy leader offered a broad smile.

"Ah, Diana Sheen, you will finally understand how completely you have been outplayed. Right now, my people are in your headquarters, breaking into your systems, learning all your secrets, and taking the things you treasure. And your personal doom approaches." Behind him, a cluster of four drones arranged in a diamond formation swung into sight from behind a building. They slowed as they neared and stopped about ten yards away. Gun barrels were very visible on their undersides. He didn't look at them and merely kept his gaze trained on hers.

He shook his head in faux sadness, giving her the condescending look she'd seen so often on the faces of those who thought themselves superior to her—and, usually, superior to everyone. "The rest of your team will join you shortly in whatever afterlife you believe in. Goodbye, Diana Sheen."

Lechnas took a step back and the whine of the drones' rotors increased. She readied a shield but assumed that anyone who was sufficiently clever to plan this ambush would be smart enough to load anti-magic. There were a couple of heavy steel sheets nearby among the debris and she reached for them with her telekinesis and drew them slowly toward her so as to not alert him.

The shout over the comm startled her and she flinched and dragged the metal to her in a single yank. "Take this, bastard!"

Diana had no idea what Kayleigh was talking about until a rocket of some kind flashed over her head and impacted the first drone, which crashed into the others and caused them all to explode. She hid under her stack of broken car pieces while flaming wreckage rained down. When she emerged the drones had gone, Cara and Rath converged on her position from either side, and Lechnas sprawled on the ground with a bloody face and a large shard from a drone protruding from his shoulder.

He rose, yanked the projectile from his flesh, and hurled it aside. His former calm arrogance had vanished, replaced by a cold rage. "You humans are vermin. The lowest of the low, barely sufficient to be our servants. For too long, we have pretended to a partnership driven by those who rule Oriceran in name only. But those of us who truly hold the power know the truth of you."

Silence filled the moment after his vitriol until Rath quipped, "Sorry. Bored. Fell asleep. You say something?" The wizard reddened with rage as the trio launched their attacks.

Diana cleared the path before them with a force blast that flung debris out of the way. It put her a step behind Cara, who angled to the left as she drew Demon and Angel from their sheaths and hurled them at his face. Lechnas batted them away with a sweep of an arm that opened him for her attack, and she stabbed Fury forward to pierce his bicep and triceps and the blade emerged from the other side. A flicker of metal sparkled in her vision and one of

Rath's blades sliced where a gap existed between his helmet and his armor to trace a line that promptly filled with blood.

She wrenched at the sword but couldn't get it free, and the attack she'd anticipated materialized. Shadow tentacles strained toward her from every separate piece of the artifact armor. There were so many that she was immediately trapped, and these were stronger and more determined than any she'd faced before. Her struggles were useless but she had a plan. First, she activated the emergency shield charm in her bracer, and it pushed out enough that she could breathe. She had the sense that it was weakening from the moment it appeared, but that was all she needed to activate the anti-tentacle charm.

Teacher and student had spent several hours discussing how to cope with the appendages. They'd agreed a magical weapon was the best choice, but as hers was currently stuck in the bastard's arm, that option was literally out of reach. Knowing such a situation might be possible, they'd come up with another idea. It was essentially a prism for magic which allowed her to shove all her power into one point, where it would collect before exploding in all directions as a series of tiny but wickedly sharp spikes. In their tests, the tentacles were shredded most of the time. The only risk was hitting the wrong people, but she hadn't seen any innocents, and both Rath and Cara were far enough away that any injuries should be minor. Hopefully. There was no real way to tell.

And no more time to worry about the possible consequences. She ignored the fact that her writhing captors now lifted her off her feet and channeled her magic into the charm, first in a trickle, then a flow, then a stream, and finally, a wide river—all that she could give. It detonated without sound and bright shards attacked the encroaching darkness and blasted it away. She landed in a crouch and grinned at Lechnas's stunned face.

"Yeah, the problem with power is that it can never stand against enough people working together." She yanked at her sword with all the power she could put into her telekinesis, and it ripped free. The shock caused the last of the tendrils around her to fail and fall away. Two knives flew past her and her adversary slapped them aside before another two followed seconds later.

She launched a force blast at his forehead as a distraction and as he blocked it, Cara raced past and drove Angel deep into his thigh and left it embedded in his flesh when she dodged his reactive swipe. The wizard seemed to struggle to find an effective counter to the attacks, and Rhazdon's Defense began to glow again. Diana surged forward, channeled her magic through the sword, and thrust it at his chest. His eyes widened when it slipped through the armor with barely any resistance and into his body with none at all. His face froze in a mask of utter disbelief and he toppled slowly without even a gurgle of protest.

Diana withdrew her sword, and Cara retrieved her dagger. They stared at each other without speaking for a moment before her second in command laughed. "Please tell me there are no more Rhazdon-inspired assholes waiting in the wings. Because I think we've had our share."

Any reply she might have made was cut short when three notable things happened at once. First, Rhazdon's

Defense shimmered and vanished to leave a much less impressive-looking enemy sprawled in death. Second, the sound of a distant explosion rumbled from the direction of the downtown. Third, Kayleigh shouted, "Drones incoming. Hightail it to the truck."

CHAPTER THIRTY-FOUR

Lechnas's defeat rippled through the enemy troops and caused a mass exodus that Kayleigh watched with her eye in the sky. The comm was filled with relieved chatter from those outside and her own yells for them to return faster. The dots that represented the Chinese drones on her map were less than thirty seconds away when the agents scrambled into the truck.

Diana was the last to enter, and as she palmed the door closed, the vehicle was already in motion. She ordered briskly, "Hank, choose somewhere we can go fast and use the weapons—probably the Parkway. At this time of night, it should be reasonably empty. Nowhere with tunnels as we'd be fish in a barrel for armed drones."

His voice was calm and relaxed. "Got it. We'll head around downtown and swing north."

The tech added the map and the truck's external cameras to the agents' displays. She naturally didn't include Hank, who was driving or Deacon, who had control of his own gear. There were sounds of concern, but they were universally more, "How do we shoot those bastards," than, "We'll all die," which was reassuring. Moving had bought them a little time, but they only had fifteen seconds before the drones would be in range to make things difficult.

The truck swayed as Hank swung abruptly left to avoid someone entering from an on-ramp. "People in this town do not know how to merge," he muttered and pulled into the required lane. "Smoke out." A whir from above marked the turret rotating to present the smoke tube. She wasn't sure if he did it to keep other vehicles at a distance or in hopes of messing with the drones.

Deacon thought along the same lines, apparently. "You did that for fun," he accused him.

She could hear the smile in the driver's voice. "Nah. It had a purpose. One day, you'll be experienced enough to understand." He shifted to serious. "Someone needs to take manual control of the guns. Who's the best shooter?" Everyone in the back turned to look at Tony.

He stroked his mustache and looked pleased with the acknowledgment. "All right. Let's do it."

Hank commanded, "Ralph, assign offensive turret to Agent Ryan."

The AI replied, "Acknowledged."

"Ralph, assign defensive turret to Agent Dornan."

Kayleigh blinked in surprise as the AI confirmed the order. A set of targeting options appeared in her display. She toggled them so the system would recognize her flight stick as the primary interface and mapped her trigger to the stun gun and her top button to the canister launcher.

The first drone to appear fell before it could fire, a

victim of Tony's mini-gun. He shouted in triumph but cut off when another dozen appeared.

"It seems you upset them by killing their leader, Boss," Cara remarked.

"I think they simply dislike trolls," Diana replied. Rath laughed and stuck his tongue out at her.

The next four attackers flew in formation at different heights and spread out so a single blast couldn't catch them. They launched their rockets as an opening salvo at the moment that they entered maximum range, and the eight smaller targets appeared on her display. The mini-gun obliterated two in the first second, followed quickly by three more. The tech twitched the stun cannon to the left and fired to destroy two more. The last impacted against a concrete bridge as the truck barreled beneath it, entirely too close for comfort.

The mobile armory's weapons had a longer range than the guns on the drones, so she fired continuously until they were all eliminated. Deacon made a strangled noise and Hank breathed a heartfelt, "Damn," but there was no opportunity to regroup or make another plan as the rest of the drones swooped in. They annihilated them in the same way as they had before and this time, caught all the missiles. Unfortunately, two operators were smart and dropped the birds below the cannons' deflections. Stun blasts peppered the truck.

"We can handle it for a while," Hank advised, "but eventually, they'll overload the systems with that much electricity. We'll need to launch our drone."

Diana shook her head, ice in her tone. "No, Hank. I think we'll take this one out personally." She pointed at

Cara and Anik. "Rifles and AP." The second in command handed the weapons and the red striped magazines out, and the three teammates turned to face the back of the truck, their weapons raised.

Cara ordered, "Sloan, come over here and get a grip on Anik and I. Rath, you hold on to him. Diana can fly, so we won't worry about her."

They repositioned in seconds, and Diana instructed, "Ralph, open the back doors." As soon as they parted, the rifles chattered. The drones tried frantically to evade the barrage and collided before they plunged downward, emitting a plume of smoke. None of the agents noticed because their eyes were all on the much larger plume of smoke in downtown.

The one that marked where their headquarters had been.

Kayleigh saw it on the truck's cameras. Their building was now rubble and emergency vehicles surrounded it. The truck swayed as Hank eased toward the north, and once it was stabilized, she magnified the view. It was completely gone but fortunately, none of the surrounding structures seemed damaged beyond broken windows.

"Well, I guess we know where the crazy witch's explosives went," Tony quipped. "The first crazy witch, that is." His heart wasn't in it, though, and it fell flat.

The tech was unashamed to feel tears well at the corners of her eyes and trickle down her face. Her mind sputtered denials but her spirit knew it was true. Their time in the place she'd learned to call home was over.

Her boss confirmed it with steel in her tone. "Ralph, alert Agent Bates. We'll activate Project Adonis."

CHAPTER THIRTY-FIVE

Diana's footsteps echoed oddly as she walked through the wide hallway of one of the vimana's lower levels. When they'd made it to Hampton Roads, Virginia, and met up with the team from ARES DC, she'd had no idea where they would be headed next.

If someone had informed her in advance that the answer was Antarctica, she would have laughed and told them to quit messing around.

But, sure enough, the ARES teams were now together at the planet's southern pole, hidden in a giant magical city that could also supposedly fly. She didn't see a situation where that would be useful for her team but supposed it was a good thing to have in one's back pocket. The place was beautiful in an archaic kind of way, and Senator Johnston had informed them that the necessary inflow of magic needed to keep it running was being "taken care of." He'd also assured her that since ARES was officially no longer part of the government, they'd be able to take on far more critical challenges than before and in a much wider variety of locations.

She'd offered the proper responses and planted a smile on her face while he'd explained their new circumstances. The oversight committee had shut them down as Finley predicted, but plans had been in the works since the organization's founding to deal with such an event. The senator had laughed and pronounced, "The people who make up the government can be extremely short-sighted sometimes. It's up to folks like us to keep an eye on the target and do what's necessary to ensure we achieve it."

He'd promised they'd have a few weeks—maybe even a month or two—to acclimate to the new situation. "Assuming nothing crazy happens like an alien invasion or something." She had the impression he was at least somewhat serious, but she wasn't prepared to deal with any problems at the moment.

Rath walked beside her, as happy as could be with the new base of operations. During the week since the battle against Lechnas, he'd had a throwing range constructed, organized a tournament—that he won—and talked about a ninja warrior style obstacle course in addition to it. *Gymnastics and throwing knives. What could go wrong?*

There was certainly enough space for any training areas they wanted to build in the lightly occupied city. The other agents dealt with the move at their own pace, and Johnston had provided additional magical staff to assist in portaling to various location to wind up affairs in Pittsburgh and DC. The senator had also arranged for her parents and Lisa to go on separate government-funded vacations to keep them out of harm's way while the agents assessed the fallout from the attacks.

It was possible they'd need to relocate to the vimana for their own safety. She was alternately all for the idea and completely against it. *Seriously, who wants to work with their parents, even if they are awesome?* Her best friend, though, would definitely come down as soon as she thought of a way to convince her.

They peered in through the glass panes as they passed the labs. Kayleigh and Deacon were still geeking out over the gear Johnston's team had quietly made vanish from official records and transferred to the facility. All the agents were stoked about the quantity, quality, and variety of equipment as well as the seemingly limitless possibilities ahead. Each of them had wanted to make a difference and for a while, they'd thought that meant one tiny corner of the world.

Now, their mandate extended to the whole planet.

She traded a fist-bump with Rath as he headed off to his quarters, which were next to hers. He grinned. "I'll be back."

His Terminator impression is improving. She merely shook her head and said, "Yeah, right, good luck finding Sarah Connor." His laughter made her happy as it always did. The other thing that always made her happy waited beyond her own door. Bryant was working in the front room of their combination apartment and private office. It had made sense to share space once they were finally in the same city —even a magical one surrounded by penguins—and no one seemed to have a problem with it. Actually, at the moment, no one had a problem with anything. It was glorious.

Diana perched on the edge of the desk. "Whatcha doin'?"

He sighed, stretched, and looked at her with a grin. "Reading through the extended version of Adonis. They have so much planned for us to do and against things we've never seen before. Even on the inside, we weren't aware of the incredible variety of magical threats to the planet."

"That's why we have bounty hunters, right?" She shrugged.

"Yeah, no. Aside from the Brownstones, I'm not sure any individual would be able to deal with this garbage if it shows up. It'll take a team, for sure."

She pushed his chair out with a foot, dropped onto his lap, and put her arms around his neck. "Well, it just so happens I know where we can get one. But it'll cost you. My people don't come cheap."

He kissed her, gently at first but that changed fairly quickly. When he broke contact, he asked, "How much are we talking?"

Diana laughed and stood, held his hand, and hauled him behind her toward the room that held the large bed she'd portaled out to retrieve. "I'm a reasonable person. But it'll probably take us hours to work the whole thing out." She grinned at him over her shoulder, happy, secure, and as stress-free as she'd been in months. "Let the negotiations commence."

The End

Please see the Authors' notes for details on the future adventures of the Federal Agents of Magic!

While this story has ended, there are still plenty of stories to tell. Look for the next series, Scion of Magic, to start releasing later this year! If you enjoyed the series, please leave a review on the books. They really help me out!

CONNECT WITH TR CAMERON

Stay up to date on new releases and fan pricing by signing up for my newsletter. CLICK HERE TO JOIN.

Or visit: www.trcameron.com/Oriceran to sign up.

If you enjoyed this book, please consider leaving a review. Thanks!

Thank you for reading the *eighth* book in the Federal Agents of Magic series, and for continuing on to the author notes! I am grateful every single day that you make it possible for me to share stories with you.

Life has had some ups and downs since the last time I sat down to write some author notes. I always get a little out of sorts as school starts up again, maybe memories from my childhood, maybe just the feeling that the summer has passed by and I didn't accomplish everything I wanted to.

But on the upside, my daughter has started playing soccer, which was my sport long ago. It's great to see her out there with the team. Sure, a little more knowledge of the actual rules would help, but it's a process, right?

So, big ending to this book, right? This was long planned as a transition point to the second large arc in the series, which sees the agents less focused on defending a specific spot and more focused on fighting off bigger enemies. It felt like a natural progression at the start, and still does, given how their powers have grown.

But Diana and company are going to have to wait a bit to get into it with those larger magical threats.

I'm a believer in the idea of creative wells – that creators of whatever kind have a reservoir that gets emptied over time and requires refilling. Different people have different means of replenishing it – some vacation, some take time off from one form of art and turn to another.

My well for Diana and her team needs refreshing. So *my* solution is to switch to a different series for a while. The new one will keep some of the most enjoyable elements of this series – strong characters, snark and humor, some fights, explorations of magic – and add in fun new elements as the main character comes to terms with her growing powers and the mysteries that surround her ancestry and her home.

Once I've spun out those, it's my intention to return to this series, as I love the characters and think the bigger picture arc will be super fun. If you'd like to keep updated on this series and on the next, opt-in to my weekly updates at www.trcameron.com/oriceran .

On a total side note: if you're into dystopian stories and video games, I can't recommend *Detroit: Become Human* highly enough. The gameplay is kind of strange if you're new to this type of game like I am, but the story is brutal. Awesome, but brutal.

Until next time, Joys upon joys to you and yours – so may it be.

The end of one great story from T.R. Cameron – just in time for the start of a new one. Soon, you will get to meet Cali, a half-Atlantean in the Oriceran Universe who works in the Double Dragons Tavern. Little does she know, a great adventure is about to start...

It's about this time of year that I always get an email from the 10Q project – an online creation that is timed around the Jewish New Year and thankfully, lets anyone join in. They ask 10 questions every year – one each day for 10 days until Rosh Hashana. Thousands participate, putting down what was most significant about the past year, what changed us, what do we hope for the next year. Then, those answers are locked away for an entire year.

Just before the project starts again (which is soon if you want to join in), you get your answers back to review. I read mine this year and thought – you had no idea what was coming or how much you'd be changing. When I wrote the answers, I still had a day job (basically, I was working two full-time jobs) and my oldest sister, Diana was still alive. I wrote that I expected the next year to be pretty calm. Nothing seemed to be on the horizon, really, one way or the other.

Okay, I was wrong. Great things happened – both good and bad – and I ended up learning how to lean into the storm and keep asking, what are you here to teach me. Some days I marveled at how painful just existing can seem and others I marveled at how an internal storm can suddenly pass.

What I forgot was that even when we don't see it, the next great adventures are already taking root and shooting tender green plants toward the surface. Things are always in a process of unfolding, getting on with things, changing into something else. My main job is to bring my willingness and be a part of it without trying to control it, even when it's difficult or even when it's so good it's a kind of scary too.

This past year that I didn't predict taught me a lot about myself – my resilience, what I really wanted, and a reminder to say no occasionally as well as yes. Soon, I'll start getting questions from 10Q and contemplating what was, what is, and what I think is coming. This time, I'll answer with a little more wisdom and be more open to what I just can't see – yet. More adventures to follow.

JOIN THE ORICERAN UNIVERSE FAN GROUP ON FACEBOOK!